One Hit Wonder

Denyse Cohen

CRIMSON
ROMANCE
Avon, Massachusetts

Published by
Crimson Romance
an imprint of F+W Media, Inc.
10151 Carver Road, Suite 200
Blue Ash, Ohio 45242

www.crimsonromance.com

POD ISBN 10: 1-4405-5064-6
POD ISBN 13: 978-1-4405-5064-5
eISBN-10: 1-4405-5063-8
eISBN-13: 978-1-4405-5063-8

Dedication

FOR JANNY AND SARAH,

WHOSE LIGHT WILL SHINE IN MY HEART

FOREVER.

Acknowledgments

Thanks to my husband, Scott, for standing by me.

To my son, Shay, for inspiring me.

To my sister, Dylene, for laughing with me.

To my best friend, Lea, for believing in me.

And to the amazing Jennifer Lawler, for saying yes.

I also want to thank family and friends who, at some point in my journey, have given me words of encouragement and support.

I praise all of you because you've made the choice to reach out and, selflessly, give something positive to someone else. If more people did that the world would be so very different.

Chapter 1

Oh, holy mother of God!

Audrey lifted both hands to her temples and tried to squeeze her head together. It felt like her skull had been opened with a dull handsaw, her brain removed, chopped, and deep-fried.

She struggled to unglue her eyelids and it took her thirty minutes to strain herself out of bed and walk toward the bathroom as upright as a caveman. The pain in her stomach was so intense she had to squeeze her abdomen with one hand while holding her head with the other.

I've never got this sick from vodka, she thought. Then she saw an empty bottle on her bathroom sink. I guess I've never drunk a whole bottle before. She threw the bottle in the trash bin beside the sink, dumped the pitcher of bloody marys that already started to smell like rotten tomatoes down the drain, and splashed cold water on her face.

After slowly making her way to the kitchen, she placed a kettle filled with water on the stove. The sun coming through the window made the bisque-colored countertop glisten as if infused with gold. Chamomile tea seemed gentler than coffee on her battered stomach, and the lack of caffeine was amended by a couple of aspirins and orange juice.

"Good morning," she said when her roommate walked in the kitchen. She could tell when Steve had gone partying the night before, because his hairdo would meld into a rubber-sole helmet the next morning. He religiously spent a good deal of money on styling products to mold his thin hair into the spiked look he seemed to like so much.

"Mornin'." He walked straight to the coffee maker and, noticing it hadn't been touched, let out a groan of unhappiness.

"Sorry. I'm drinking tea. Want some?" She was leaning against the counter with her favorite mug, a panda bear and bamboo leaves hand-painted by a giggly Japanese seven-year-old.

He made a face of disgust, started the coffee pot and, sitting down at the table, said, "Rough night, huh?"

Instinctively she straightened her back and smoothed her hair. Is it obvious?

Steve glanced at her and smiled. The coffee maker burbled away as he pressed the buttons on his Blackberry.

"You got loads of sympathizers on Facebook," he said without looking away from the phone.

"Mm?"

"Yep, twenty-three comments and seventeen likes."

"Oh, shit." She had completely forgotten about it. Last night, after she'd arrived home with vodka and bloody mary mix for dinner, she had updated her Facebook: I was laid-off from the worst job ever, so why does it still feels like a kick in the gut?

"It grants you top news status. More than likely, every time anyone you know logs in, it will be the first thing they see." He seemed proud of himself.

"Fantastic!" She scratched her head and her long hair went wild.

"Did you go see your friend's band yesterday?"

"They're playing tonight."

"You stayed home and got hammered by yourself?" Steve shook his head. "Bummer."

"Hey, I don't need your sympathy. I like to be alone."

He was fixing himself a cup of coffee when a woman emerged from the hall and stood on the threshold of the kitchen. Blonde and tanned, she looked like a cast-off from The Real Housewives of Beverly Hills. Audrey wasn't surprised; Steve's specialty was hooking up with older woman who turned out to be jealous-going-on-possessive, like toddlers unable to share their toys. He had his back to the woman, turning only when Audrey had said hello and received a thin-lipped smile in response.

"Good morning, Rebecca," he said, walking toward the woman and giving her a peck on the lips.

Rebecca grunted a good morning that sounded a lot like you son of a bitch.

"This is my roommate. Audrey, Rebecca. Rebecca, Audrey."

"You didn't tell me your roommate was a girl."

Steve looked at Audrey with an apologetic expression.

Okay now, just because you're old doesn't make me a "girl."

Audrey flipped her hair to the side and stretched her arms above her head, revealing a sliver of midriff.

"Sure am," she intoned, adjusting the hem of her shorts and slowly sliding her hands down her thighs, strong from playing soccer every year from second grade through high school. The hint of worry in Steve's eyes filled her with satisfaction, as it indicated Rebecca fitted the profile.

"I'm going to take a long hot bath. Stevie, we'll finish this later, okay?" Audrey said, sliding her fingers down his arm as she squeezed herself between them and walked away. Midway to her bedroom, she peeked over her shoulder and saw Steve chugging his coffee as Rebecca stared him down furiously.

On the bed, she opened her laptop and discovered he wasn't just messing with her. Facebook indeed had twenty-three comments of condolences for her lost job. Some people shared similar stories, which didn't make her feel any better. She wondered if it had been a good idea to make her situation known. She was venting, not probing for pity. What was there to "like"? she wondered as she puzzled over the number next to the thumbs-up icon. Her mood scurried from irritation to sadness to misery, and she let out a big breath; pushing the hot air out until her belly stuck to her back, then went into the shower to sulk.

Chapter 2

Childhood friends, Audrey and Matt had lost contact after junior high. Now that they were Facebook friends, she found it hard to associate the man on Matt's profile picture with the boy she used to know. He had become a husky guy, a bearded grizzly bear with kind eyes. They shared snapshots of life that often became long threads of conversation about bits of the past, punctuated by lonesome interjections from other people who'd soon fall back into silence as if laughing at a joke without understanding the punch line.

The coming night would be the first time they had seen each other in person in three years and only the second time since he moved away. Timing couldn't be more perfect. She needed to remember life was once as straightforward and clear as a shot of vodka. She was happy to reencounter a friend from her preadolescent years; it meant their relationship remained untainted by the sexual intricacies of opposite-sex friendships. In the steam of the shower, she pondered about the benefits and detriments of sex and money in her life; for a while now, she had neither.

*

"Audrey, I can't believe you've made it!" Matt walked toward her with his arms open.

It had taken him a few minutes to make his way to the bar, but she enjoyed watching the band talking to their fans, because as artists became famous they also became inaccessible to the people who had made them so.

"I wouldn't miss it for the world." Meeting a beloved friend who played in a rock band seemed to be a treacherous plot. Her last relationship had sunk like a hollowed ship, and the messy break-up with the angered boyfriend made her vow to stay away from all matters of the heart until she drafted an internal map from which she could navigate through love. Thus, her celibacy had gone on for close to half of a year. In that time, she hadn't met anyone who had substance or was not only trying to get inside her pants.

"Let me look at you." Matt twirled her around. "You still look good." She was wearing a sweater dress that hugged her body, a jean jacket, scarf, and knee-high black boots. Not her most original ensemble, but a comfortable yet dressy option to her favorite—Levi's.

"You, too." She grabbed his black-bearded cheeks and gave them a squeeze in an elderly-aunt fashion. "You look so cute," she said, as if talking to a five-year-old.

"Cute? You know what cute really means, don't you? Ugly dressed up. Three rungs below handsome."

"No, it doesn't. You goof."

The rest of the band joined them at bar. "You remember the guys, don't you?" Matt asked.

"Absolutely." She shook hands with Tyler, John, and Kevin.

"And here's our latest addition. Rob the grip man. Rob, Audrey. Audrey, Rob."

"Nice to meet you." She extended her hand to Rob while Matt turned to the bartender and ordered a round of tequila shots.

He handed each a glass. "To the next gig and friendships."

Clearly, she wasn't the only friend the band had in town; they had occupied an entire corner of the pub, having several tables joined together.

Matt gulped his shot and nodded toward his bandmates. "What do you think of coming with us?"

"Yeah, right," she chuckled. "Thanks, Matt. But I don't really need a vacation right now."

"Just hear me out. We're getting ready to record a CD when these gigs are over and we'll need promotional material and a new website. We have no real photographs of the band, and with your background I think you can be our photographer. " He took a slug of beer and met her dubious gaze. "See? Although it might seem like a spur-of-the-moment invitation, we've thought it through."

"We?" The smile she kept on her face for most of the night shattered and disappeared.

"The band. We discussed it after I've read on Facebook you got laid off. It works out perfectly." Matt caught himself. "Sorry, by the way."

"The band?" Her surprise was quickly escalating to anxiety, followed by a sudden need of tequila. Having her business discussed by other people had never been how she handled her problems. She made a mental note to beware of social networks.

"Listen, we plan to make the most professional CD we can. Since selling music online has become way simpler, we need to move out of Myspace and we—"

"Matt, that is great, truly. I mean, I think your sound is amazing, you definitely got what it takes to grow. But if you want to make a professional CD, website, and whatever, shouldn't you hire a professional photographer?"

"Well, it's not just the obvious money reason. Hey, we'd like to have someone with us to photograph the tour. You know, a candid portraits sort of thing?"

She stared at him, expressionless.

"Who is better to be in a bus with five guys than a hot girl?"

Oh, goodness. She recoiled as if she had been just slapped on the face.

"I'm teasing. I'm teasing." He patted her shoulder. "You know you're like an annoying little sister to me."

"I'm older."

"Oh, bollocks. Seven months doesn't count. I'm more mature."

"Did you just say bollocks?" Audrey shook her head. "You can take a rock star out of the nerd, but you can't take the nerd out . . . wow . . . . stop." She tried to shield her ribs with her elbows as Matt tickled her.

He obliged and straightened himself. "But seriously think about it, will ya? There is even a little salary involved; uh, more like a stipend, and we will take care of expenses."

"Thanks, Matt, I'll think about it."

Chapter 3

It was a no-brainer decision: she was unemployed and had found a gig to pay the bills. Nothing ominous about it. The tour would take two months; after it she would return and pick up her life from where she'd left off. Then why she couldn't shake the feeling this was not a good idea?

Her concerns branched out in opposite directions, like cartoony versions of her good and evil selves floating above her shoulders and fighting over what she should do. Her good side worried about Matt's feelings. Although he had said out loud he considered her an annoying little sister, he could be saying one thing but secretly hoping for another. She was happy to have found him again, but after their second meeting she was sure there was no spark.

You can't do this. Get out while you can, her evil self warned with a screechy voice that lifted the hairs on her neck. She had never crossed the line between a hobbyist photographer and a hired one. Not only would she would be judged for her work, but she would be held accountable for it. There couldn't be a change of plans or loss of interest, the two primary reasons that kept her from achieving anything in life. She would have to stick with it until the end and that scared her shitless.

*

"At least I don't have to explain to my lady friends I'm not involved with the Brazilian knock-out I happen to live with." Steve said when Audrey told him she was breaking her lease.

"I'm not Brazilian, but I'm glad I can help."

"Half-Brazilian. You know what I mean: deep olive skin, long wavy hair, nice popozão."

Audrey darted a vicious look toward him. "You know I hate that word."

"I know." He chuckled.

"The fact that you mention it doesn't say much about you, does it? It was bad enough to like Kevin Federline in 2006, but still listen to this awful song four years later."

"I don't listen to it! I just remember it. A homage to my dear friend."

"Charming." She sighed in disgust.

"What are you going to do when the tour is over?"

"I don't know, but I'll kill myself before I take another secretarial job. Can't live inside a cubicle hypnotized by fluorescent lights and addicted to bad coffee anymore."

"Maybe you can go back to school; your mother would love it," Steve said.

"I don't know. Grad school is expensive. I don't feel like adding another twenty grand to my student debt, regardless of the opportunities a master's degree might bring. Maybe I'll go back to Japan . . . or somewhere else." She'd spent a quite enjoyable year teaching English to children in Japan. Except the job didn't give her any invaluable skills back in America, where almost everyone already spoke English. Still, she had learned to surf and it made her year abroad magnificent.

"If you need a place, you can always come back."

"How about your lady friends?"

"Let them think you're competition. It gets them more motivated in bed."

"Oh, please."

"Remember Rebecca? She became a gymnast after she saw you. She even had to go to a chiropractor the next day to re-align her spine."

"No way." Audrey bawled with laughter.

"I'm dead serious. It was fucking fantastic—literally."

"You're bad."

"That's why they like me."

*

Matt gave her the low-down on how the tour worked; their manager, Bill, had rented a RV (a.k.a tour bus). The band and the crew (she and Rob) would travel from one city to the next until the last gig in Austin, Texas. Then they would drive straight home, unless Bill booked something on the way. Some gigs were nearly back-to-back, a Friday night somewhere and Saturday night somewhere else. Rob was the official tour bus driver, but all the band members would have to help him to keep up with the schedule.

They were leaving in two weeks.

"These are blessings, minha filha." Isabel, Audrey's mother, believed being laid off and Matt's invitation were the workings of guiding angels leading her to professional fulfillment and everlasting happiness. However, Audrey's skepticism, despite her mother's religious fervor, allowed her to believe only in the power of DSL.

The band was going to detour to pick her up. She didn't quite like the idea because it made her think of a hitchhiking hippie smoking pot in a baby blue VW van. The word "groupie" also crossed her mind, and as a guide she watched Almost Famous three times that week. She wanted to learn from Penny Lane, but the woman contradicted herself and paid for it dearly. Instead of following her own advice: never take it seriously, never get hurt, Penny fell for the guitarist and tried to killed herself after seeing the spineless jerk with his girlfriend. However, Audrey learned something from Elaine, the overprotective mother—Be bold, and mighty forces will come to your aid.

Bold was a word she hadn't said or thought about it in ages; she spent countless hours trying to remember her last bold action. Almost three years ago, she found a job teaching English to children in Japan. It was the last risk she had taken, and perhaps the reason she thought about it so often. She couldn't pinpoint when her life had made the turn to fuck-up-land. At last, she was being bold again.

*

You've got to be kidding me, Audrey thought, as she watched the old RV turning the corner of the street. The Winnebago's brakes shrieked as it halted in front of her and she looked embarrassedly over her shoulders, hoping none of the neighbors were watching. It wasn't much of a plan to begin with, and this had been the first mistake. The vehicle was not a century old, but it was from the last century: faded paint, avocado-green pinstripes chipped away at the edges, duct tape on the rearview mirror. She should probably get out of here as soon as possible, turn and walk back inside the house, but it was too late.

Even after strictly forbidding her parents to leave the house, she twitched with hope her father would come out and forbid her to travel across the country inside an unsafe vehicle. When she glanced toward the window, he was laughing hysterically—convulsion-attack style. Her mother stood beside him, waving one hand and covering her mouth with the other. She wasn't sixteen anymore; she could no longer count on her parent's overprotection. Audrey exhaled deeply, as though blowing out smoke, and her shoulders sank so low, she could have brushed the sidewalk with the tip of her fingers.

Like a B-movie spaceship, short only of dry-ice fog and neon lights, the Winnebago's door opened slowly. Except the humanoid that appeared, with his hand up, signaling he'd come in peace wasn't alien.

"Hi." Matt's smile was as big and as innocent as Sesame Street's Ernie.

"Hi." Audrey waved back. "So this is the tour bus, huh?"

"Yeah, how do you like it?" He stood beside her and they both stared at the Winnebago.

"It's interesting."

"It might not scream rock-and-roll, but it beats actual bus seats."

"I can imagine it."

Matt leaned closer and lowered his voice as if telling her a secret. "We have a full-size bed."

Audrey rolled her eyes and threw her back-pack over her shoulders while Matt picked up her duffle bag.

"Wait," Isabel hollered, coming down the driveway with, Audrey guessed, a tin of cookies.

"Mom!" She widened her eyes. "I told you to stay inside," she murmured crossly as Isabel approached them.

Isabel ignored her and walked toward Matt. "Matt, Oh my goodness. Look how big you are." She lifted her arm around his shoulder and kissed his cheek.

"Hello, Mrs. Whitman," he said shyly.

"Look at this beard." She ran her hand along the side of his face. "You were twelve the last time I saw you. You are so handsome." She turned to Audrey. "Isn't he handsome?"

"Audrey thinks I'm cute."

"Nonsense, you're handsome," Isabel reassured him.

Isabel's hand was still on Matt's face when her attention pivoted to a man coming out of the Winnebago. Lean and tall, he had tentacles of blond hair framing a long face, lit by fluorescent green eyes. After him, a man with brown hair, full lips, and arms that stretched the sleeves of his shirt. He was followed by a square-jawed man with honey eyes and wide shoulders, the tallest of the washboard-abs-type trio.

Isabel stepped to Audrey's side and muttered, "Oh my."

Audrey looked away and, clearing her throat, said inconspicuously, "Wait, there's one more." At that moment, another man, older than the others came out, a balding version of Michael Madsen.

She imagined what her mother would be thinking; she had wondered about it herself.

"I'm glad your father decided to stay inside," Isabel whispered, squeezing Audrey's hand.

"Mom, meet Kevin, Tyler, John, and Rob." Audrey introduced them in the order they had exited the Winnebago.

"Nice to meet you," Isabel said. The men replied politely, then lapsed into silence.

"Okay." Audrey turned to her mom. "We have to go, the band has a schedule. That's why I've asked you to stay inside."

"All right. You guys drive safe now."

"Don't worry, Mrs. Whitman, Rob is a professional." Matt tapped Rob's shoulder as they hustled back inside the bus.

"Very good, then. Oh, wait. I've made you cookies for the trip."

"Thanks, Mom," Audrey said, reaching for the tin without a trace of enthusiasm.

"Thanks, Mrs. Whitman." Matt grabbed it from Audrey's hand, leaned to give Isabel a kiss, and moved away opening the tin and stuffing a cookie in his mouth.

Isabel rubbed Audrey's arm, and hugged her. "You have fun now. Call me and tell me everything."

"I will," Audrey said, biting her lower lip.

"And stop worrying so much. When I was your age, I would have given an arm to be inside that. . . ." She looked over Audrey's shoulder. ". . . RV?"

"It's a tour bus, Mom."

"Right on."

Chapter 4

Audrey wondered if hanging out with musicians would be like hanging out with the band. Was this how rock stars did it? Well, maybe rock stars on a budget that partied in camp sites, roadside hotels, and rundown pubs across the East Coast. Most of the time, she felt in her teens again, except she could legally drink, and so she did—a lot.

The truth was, the alcohol helped to drown her worries. She took a million pictures, hoping quantity would give her a cushion to relax. If ten percent of the photographs were average and one percent was excellent, more pictures could save her from embarrassment when the tour was over. The internet was a wonderful resource for inspiration. Everyone is a photographer now, she thought while browsing on Flickr. Her models were cooperative and, for the most part, she didn't bother them much.

The bulk of her work consisted of positioning her tripod around the stage during the performances. Light was her fierce enemy; she could never shoot with a flash, afraid it would disturb the band or the audience. It wouldn't matter, anyway, her shoe-mount flash wasn't strong enough to light the entire stage. She liked the mood in the photographs, colored only by the dim lights of the pubs, although foggy faces hardly made for good marketing material.

*

"Let me take some pictures of you." Kevin grabbed her camera from a table at a fast-food restaurant connected to the gas station they'd stopped at in North Carolina.

"No." Audrey shook her head adamantly and reached for the camera. Kevin ducked away and Audrey gave up, not wanting to inflict the innocent patrons of The Biscuit House to a cat-and-mouse chase. Surely, the elderly couple splitting and buttering their biscuits in unison at a table by the window wasn't interested in the mayhem-with-gravy combo.

"Cut it out, Kevin. You might break her camera." Matt paid for the bag of biscuits he was taking back to the bus. He was always attentive and, most importantly, truthful to his words, which meant no sexual vibe between them. He really considered her an annoying little sister. That was a relief, although she resented the "annoying" bit.

"Audrey, you have gorgeous eyes." Kevin zoomed in the lens on her face, and she instinctively covered it with her hands.

"If you delete something, I swear." Audrey pointed a finger at him. "I haven't downloaded last night's photos yet."

"Man, give her the camera. I had my sexy shirt on last night." Tyler winked at Audrey from the soda machine as he filled his cup with Dr. Pepper. She frowned at him, trying to decode his ambiguous expression.

Two days before, his dispensed gallantries had escalated to a rubbing of her feet that felt unexpectedly sensuous.

"You have a tattoo?" Tyler gasped while studying the delicate cluster of cherry blossoms on her right ankle. His own arm appeared to portray a narrative much like Dante's *Inferno*—ergo it was hard to see authenticity in his caught breath over a few flowers.

Kevin purred, "A tattoo? You naughty girl." He nodded to Tyler to scoot over so he could sit at the little table across from her. Instead, Tyler moved to the floor, without letting go of her ankle, and started to massage her foot.

Audrey snapped her brows at him. "What are you doing?"

"Relax," Tyler told her, smirking and squeezing her foot a little harder. Kevin propped his feet on the table as he said, "I'm next." Tyler proceeded to massage her feet and calves while staring intently into her eyes. For a split second, she feared if she were alone with him inside the Winnebago it could had been the end of her perennial celibacy.

Tyler was well aware of his sex appeal and he used it well, but she dismissed his smirk as John emerged from the groceries side of the gas station with a bottle of pink lemonade and a pack of cigarettes in his hands. "You guys about ready?" he said.

"Aren't you going to eat?" Rob asked.

"I'm not hungry." John's gaze stopped at the camera in Kevin's hand as he handed it back to Audrey.

*

John was the only one who hadn't opened up to her, ignoring her as much as he could. She couldn't quite figure out why he continually froze her out, whatever it was; an interrupted look, a change of subject, walking away whenever she arrived. She wanted to knock it out of his head with a crowbar.

Acutely aware of his behavior, the only thing left to do was find out what was his problem. She was all right, wasn't she? A bit flaky and gawky at times, but she found solace in knowing she was the only one who suffered by her own faults. In truth, she considered herself quite gregarious, even witty and smart. Then, why was John being such a snob?

"Are you going to the bathroom?" Audrey asked when he got up from a folding chair near the fire and started to walk toward the bathroom at a campsite in Virginia. She needed to talk to him alone, without the others overtaking the conversation and transforming it into a big joke. They hadn't talked a lot before the tour, but it never crossed her mind he was going to be the one she'd butt heads with.

"Oh . . . yes." John turned back, surprised.

They had been making s'mores and drinking instant cappuccino with whiskey by the fire after dinner—a bag of fast-food hamburgers.

"I'll go with you." Audrey stood and walked toward him.

"Anyone else?" John said.

Kevin and Matt shook their heads, Tyler and Rob were already in their tent—the cheaper alternative to hotel rooms. She slept on the bed in the Winnebago and everyone else slept in two tents. She had offered to take turns but they refused. Sometimes Kevin or Matt slept on the couch, rarely Rob or Tyler, never John.

Audrey bit her lips to prevent a smile, amused by his eagerness not to be alone with her. Matt had told her John was their leader, the glue that kept them together from the start. Essentially, he was the sun which the band depended on to survive, providing energy and generating life; in other words, composing the songs.

"Gosh, it's cold when you're not by the fire." She rubbed her arms as they walked.

"It's actually not bad for March. It could be a lot worse." John looked straight ahead and down at the ground at each step.

"I had forgotten how much fun camping is. My father used to take me all the time when I was little."

They walked forward in semi-darkness, guided by the light hanging on the corner of the bathroom's bare cement construction.

John, with his hands in his pockets, said, "I'm glad—"

"Boo!" Kevin had sneaked up behind them and pinched Audrey's waist.

"Ahhhh!" She jumped. "You idiot!" She frantically slapped his arms as he ducked and stepped away. When she turned back to John, he was gone. She was disappointed; it was the first time in days he had spoken to her directly.

"What do you think of me and you going to explore the woods?" Kevin asked, grabbing her hand and pulling her toward a dark trail on their left.

She pulled her hand away. "Yeah, right. So I can be eaten by a Sasquatch while you run for your life."

"That hurts my feelings. You don't think I can protect you?" Kevin flexed his arms and kissed his biceps.

"It isn't a matter if you can or can't, but rather what your survival instincts will tell you to do, and I have a hunch they'll tell you to protect those golden locks of yours."

When they arrived at the bathrooms, John was already leaving.

"Johnny, Audrey thinks I would run away and let her be the entrée of a hungry Sasquatch. Can you believe it?"

"I kind of can." John lit a cigarette and wisps of smoke rose into the air.

"Oh, man! What's a guy have to do to earn some respect around here?"

"Don't feel bad, It's not just you." She stepped on the bathroom's threshold. "It's self-preservation, people think of themselves first."

John raised his eyebrows and walked away. She watched him being enveloped by darkness before closing the door.

Chapter 5

"Let's have a toast." Kevin often suggested, raising his glass. They all drank together, but no one felt like toasting every time they took a sip. So, at the later hours of the night, the communal answer was no, and they would just knock back their whiskey—Kevin's favorite—making faces and shaking their heads. He could have made a fortune as a bootlegger; whenever Audrey thought they'd finished drinking, he surfaced with another bottle. In the beginning, she wondered if he was trying to get her drunk. She eventually realized he was trying to get everyone drunk.

"Audrey, how come you don't have a boyfriend?" Kevin's flirtations were always more acute as the emptied bottles amassed.

"Who said I don't?" she said in a defiant tone. It had been almost six months since she had her last encounter with a lingering ex-boyfriend. He was someone she grew accustomed to having around but never felt compelled to take the next step with. He had hinted more than once they were heading to the altar, but when time came to make a decision, she bailed.

"Only an idiot would let a girl like you go on a two-month road trip with a bunch of guys, and you don't look like the type of girl who would put out for an idiot."

"Then your chances are zero, aren't they?"

Kevin chuckled. "I don't mind being an idiot when it comes to you." His green eyes fixed on her like laser beams ready to take her down. Fortunately, with eyelids droopy and attention dispersed, he always seemed to have had one too many drinks to use his weapons of seduction properly.

*

Sobriety hours entailed photographing the band and updating their MySpace, Facebook and Twitter accounts. At her old job, she'd spent long minutes scrolling down Facebook's news feed out of boredom. She thought it was stupid for people to describe their entire day using status updates, and was specially annoyed when someone would post "I'm going to bed, good night." Now she twittered the band's every move, no matter how silly or weird. She also set up a Tumblr account and posted behind-the-scenes pictures along with the twitter updates, increasing dramatically the number of followers in less than two weeks.

Very naturally, she started to act like a promoter when they arrived at a new location, taking the initiative to call radio stations to arrange interviews if there was enough time. Once in Asheville, she managed to get a TV appearance, orchestrated in part by the venue owner's local influence, but likely impossible without her diligence.

She also arranged for the band to visit a school that offered a music program for underprivileged kids. Peter, one of the program's volunteers came up to her in the bar where the band was playing. He was a seventeen-year-old high school senior, very determined to get into Yale in the fall. It was what got him volunteering in the first place, but he'd confessed after he met the kids he felt helping them was the biggest thing he'd ever done.

"Excuse me, are you the band's manager?" He must have assumed because of the way Audrey moved around the place before the concert, talking to the owner, pointing at the stage, and setting up a table with the band's CDs and T-shirts for sale.

Peter invited the band to come to the school to play and talk to the kids. Audrey agreed without asking the guys. He handed her his phone number and left to study for a calculus test the next morning. She stared at him walking away, and felt touched by his determination and confidence. Peter was clearly a responsible and—more importantly—compassionate young man. She thought about what she had done for others during her high school years and quivered with regret.

After the concert, she told the band about their next-day engagement and didn't have to convince anyone. During a game of pool, they decided to not trash themselves that night.

"Got to put up a fresh face for the kids." Kevin said, lifting up his beer bottle.

John shook his head and racked the balls.

"What? Beer is cool. Shots are the problem." Kevin shook his head and took another gulp. He was sitting near the pool table with Audrey, Matt, and Rob. Tyler was talking to a couple of girls at the bar.

"Can we play?" Tyler asked, bringing the two blondes over.

"Sure." John chalked his cue and broke sharply.

"This is Ashley and Tiffany." Tyler placed his beer at the table and grabbed cues for the girls. "That is John."

"Hi," the girls sing-songed.

John lifted his beer and nodded.

"Kevin, Audrey, Matt, and Rob," Tyler said, pointing at each.

"I'm on your team." Tiffany moved to John's side of the table. She was wearing a pink V-neck sweater that complemented her rosy skin and a short skirt that was very inappropriate for playing pool. Her shaggy hair fell on her face as she smiled apologetically, telling John she wasn't a very good player.

For minutes, it seemed Matt and Kevin had lost their verbal skills as they watched the game—or the blonde. Tyler and Ashley seemed to be ready to take their game elsewhere. They giggled, whispered, and hugged every time one of their balls sank. Since those girls came in a pair, Audrey suspected Tiffany would also be getting ready to move along in her game with John, and a surge of irritation rushed through Audrey, making her stand up abruptly.

Matt and Kevin turned their heads toward her, and realizing what she'd done, she said casually, "I'm going to get a drink."

"I'm packing it in." Rob stood as well. Inwardly, she sighed in relief when their gazes fell on him. Rob usually was the first one to go to bed, so he could drive the next day while the rest of the band slept in the bus.

Audrey grabbed her camera bag and walked away before Rob, afraid of being asked to return with drinks for everyone. At the bar, she ordered a beer, sat at a stool in front of the TV screen, and placed her bag on the floor under a foot rest. She sipped her beer and glanced at the pool table, Tyler was rubbing the girl's back and she felt a little jealous. It had been months since she was touched like that. Hell, six months. She turned her gaze to the other side of the bar. Perhaps, she would see someone, and she could hook up, too, if she wanted. In fact, as she looked at the pool table again, she knew could have any one of those guys. Except John. She wasn't his type. He preferred long-legged blondes.

She closed her eyes and took a long pull of beer, savoring the cool, bitter taste that coated her mouth. When she opened her eyes again, John was handing Kevin his cue and, stroking his fingers through his hair as if relieved of a heavy burden, grabbed his cigarette pack from the stool behind him and walked away. Alone. The long-legged blonde looked at the other girl and shrugged, then turned to Kevin and smiled. As Audrey watched John walking toward the door, he sneaked a sideway peek at her. She immediately felt a tantalizing warmth running through her body and, disconcerted, looked away.

*

Bill wasn't enthused over Audrey's interventions. After the first radio interview he called often. During one of those calls, John looked flustered—then suddenly relieved—as the bus stopped at a gas station and he jumped out.

"That was a good thing" and "it is free publicity," she heard him say into the phone as he stepped from the bus. She tried to appear inconspicuous as she leaned against the window. "No! She's not expecting to be paid for that." John's voice became an indecipherable mutter as he moved out of her hearing range.

Is he standing up for me? Audrey wondered, watching him pace with the phone and gesture sternly. When he hung up and walked inside the gas station, she jumped out of the bus and followed, finding him staring at soft drinks in front of a floor-to-ceiling refrigerator.

"John?" She approached him gingerly. "Is everything okay?"

"What do you mean?"

"Bill."

"Oh, it's fine. He was just asking about some of the things we've been doing."

"Does he think I'm meddling?

"Nothing he can do about it from hundreds of miles away." John snorted.

"I don't want to cause any trouble—" Audrey smiled sheepishly, "—for you."

John held her gaze and her heart skipped a beat. She felt the charged energy between them, and when he took a step in her direction, it multiplied by tenfold.

"Audrey—"

"Hey kids," Tyler said, coming out of freaking nowhere and grabbing a soda from the refrigerator. "What's happening?"

John twitched his lips at her, then turned to an expectant Tyler. "I was telling Audrey about Bill's management style."

"Stand back and watch?" Tyler shook his head in disapproval. "He never leaves his office."

"Why do you work with him?" Audrey asked, disappointed by the interruption. She thought she saw something very peculiar in John's eyes when he said her name, and she desperately wanted to know what it was.

"There are benefits." John said, looking at Tyler with an unspoken rebuke. "His studio, his connections."

"But he manages too many little bands, probably to keep his upscale lifestyle," Tyler said.

"Don't sweat it." John looked at Audrey. "Everything you're doing is great for the band's image. He'll realize it sooner or later."

"I'm not worried about Bill. In fact, I'm cool if I finish the tour without ever meeting him."

*

After Bill backed off, it felt as if they were on a road trip instead of a professional engagement. Not that the band didn't take their job seriously, because they did—especially John. He was always hauling around an old acoustic guitar, playing notes, and writing in a composition book. She even witnessed a song being born one afternoon on their way to South Carolina, when she was in the back of the bus reading *Eat, Pray, Love* and longing for pasta.

"Check this out." John straightened himself on the seat and fixed his guitar on his lap. Then he stroked his guitar and mumbled something about the wind on birch trees, dreams that fly away, and a life spent waiting.

Matt, Tyler, and Kevin geared their attention on John. Tyler got his bass and played a seamless note. Kevin sang along as John repeated the words, and Matt nodded his head rhythmically. After a few minutes of repetition, words were amended and shuffled into a chorus. Kevin sang in his high-pitched voice something about forgotten dreams.

She tried to efface herself, pretending to be completely absorbed in the book. It was the first time they had done any composing since the tour started, and she didn't want to disturb them. Awe rushed through her veins, as if she was witnessing Michelangelo carve out David from a block of marble. For a moment, she thought about college and why she had chosen to study art— the creative process was fascinating, and she loved watching the band collaborate to transform words and sounds into something meaningful. Something that could travel inside people and rip their guts apart the way songs often did shot a bolt of emotion through her veins.

A little later, she had abandoned her book and was concentrating on not throwing up when Kevin lay next to her on the bed.

"What's the matter? You don't look so good."

"Motion sickness."

"Really?"

"Yes, it ranges from a little nudge on the stomach to tsunami-scale barfing. The smell of diesel doesn't help."

"Even your foot is cold." He touched her foot with his.

Kevin had a natural way to getting close to people; somehow, he was always touching her. Normally she would feel uncomfortable, but he behaved so casually he could be giving her a handshake. She noticed he would throw his arms around the shoulders of one of the guys when walking inside a convenience store, or give them little punches when messing around. She figured it was his way of being friendly and, slowly, had started to relax to his touchy personality.

"It seems we've been behind a very smelly old truck for ages." She turned her face to him, wiping her hand across the drops of sweat on her forehead. "How much longer 'til we stop?" She squeezed her stomach, hoping to keep its contents from coming out.

"Not long." Kevin stroked her hair and called out, "Hey John?"

John stood at the doorway and looked at them.

"Can you ask Rob to stop somewhere? Audrey is sick."

"Sure."

They stopped at a gas station and she ran out of the bus barefooted, feeling immediately better by standing on firm ground. She waited in front of the bus door, taking deep breaths and listening for her body's signals. They commanded her to run. Like an arrow, she flew to the curb on the back of the convenience store. The wintery midday air scratched her bare arms and the cold cement coated the soles of her feet. Her breakfast, so delicious not more than an hour ago, was now a plate of steel wool pads traveling up her throat.

She inhaled and smoke punched her in the gut. John was standing a few feet away, holding her shoes in one hand and a cigarette in the other.

She stared at him and he followed her gaze to the hand with the cigarette—the executioner and his axe.

"Sorry." He dropped the shoes on the ground near the curb and walked away.

Her lips parted to thank him, but the words didn't come out. The smell of smoke was nauseating, and she could only focus on keeping whatever was left of her meal where it belonged. She wished John had dropped the contents of the other hand and stayed, but he never did what she expected of him. Unlike Kevin, who relied on human interaction to survive, John watched the action from the sidelines. She sensed something between them, but his behavior made it impossible for her to figure out what it was. So, looking at her shoes on the ground, it dawned on her that, with absolutely no fuss and, perhaps without even liking it, he took care of everyone—herself included.

Chapter 6

On the drive from Raleigh to Columbia, Audrey sat on the passenger's seat beside Rob. A true bohemian who'd chosen to do what he did to be exactly where he was—drinking, traveling, and listening to rock-and-roll. His girlfriend had gotten pregnant before he left for the Gulf War. They got married, then divorced a few months after he returned. His eighteen-year-old daughter seemed to be the only reason he had a job at all; everything he owned was in his rucksack.

"I did the house-with-a-yard thing when Stacey was young, so she could come over and stay with me every other weekend. When she left for college I said 'no more of this shit, man.' I don't like being stuck in one place for long. I want to see America."

He spoke of his daughter with tenderness and had made sure to be a part of her life. "I taught her how to play the guitar."

They'd planned to spend part of the summer traveling together: Nevada, Arizona, and Mexico. The trip was Stacey's idea, and it made Rob so happy he glowed when talking about it. "She wants to spend time with me." His smile cut his face from ear to ear.

The gig in Columbia, South Carolina, although happening very early on, was the highlight of the tour, at least in regards to turnout. The band was going to be part of the line-up in the city's Saint Patrick's Day festival. She'd never heard of it, but it seemed to be a quite large event, with around thirty thousand people partying in a closed-off area of downtown called Five Points.

"This is awesome," Kevin said, as John walked to the front desk to check them in into a historic brick-building hotel that used to be a bakery. The rooms were each about a hundred dollars over their budget, but proximity was important since they couldn't drive to the performance area the day of the event.

"We're probably sharing rooms, so let's keep the same arrangement in case one of us has company." The prospect of being at walking distance from a hub of partying college girls made Tyler very happy.

The "arrangement" meant the first to arrive at the Winnebago with their guest hung something at the door as a sign for the others to go sleep anywhere but there. Audrey was the most inconvenienced by it, the one without a bed for the night, and then having to find a Laundromat the next day to get the sheets washed. But since it didn't happen every night, and the boys gave her the bed exclusively on normal nights, she played along.

"How about if more than one of us has company?" Audrey said, defiantly.

She hadn't planned on having a one-night-stand in South Carolina, but she thought Tyler was very cocky to assume he was the only one who might.

Tyler, Kevin, and Matt gave her dumbfounded stares. Rob seemed to be enjoying the exchange, chuckling under his breath.

"Audrey, you slut," Kevin teased, but when they looked at him with straight faces he said, "Sorry, just kidding."

John approached them with keys in his hand. "I've got two rooms, and each have double queen beds. Rob and I can stay in the bus, Kevin and Tyler share one room, Matt and Audrey the other." He turned to Audrey and, in a surprising moment of eye contact, said, "If that's okay with you."

It took her a few seconds to gather her thoughts. His eyes were translucent, like pieces of amber, with yellow rings around the pupils, and shapely thick eyebrows that hooded his expressive eyes. A faint scar cut through his left brow, making it a little disheveled in the middle.

"Yes, of course," she said, feigning nonchalance.

"Queen beds work out great. We can double-up in case one or more of us"—Tyler looked at Audrey—"needs to use the bedroom."

"Wait—" Matt looked confused.

"Of course, we can pretty much solve the whole predicament if Audrey and I would sleep together. In the same room. Together." Kevin twisted his hands in opposite directions while tapping the tip of his fingers together.

"What predicament?" John said, a little irritated.

"Don't bother," said Matt. "Let's go, Audrey."

*

The next morning she went for a run on the streets around the hotel. Matt was sound asleep and she knew the boys had stayed up late, so it was better not to wake him. She'd called it a night around one in the morning and left them in an Irish pub a couple of blocks away.

The sun was bright, but the temperature was in the upper forties. It took only a few minutes jogging up a hilly street that led to the University of South Carolina campus for her to feel warm. She liked the wooded streets and old houses, many transformed into duplexes for students. There were old cars parked on the streets and plastic and beach chairs on the lawn, probably the preparations for the parade. Not a lot of people out, though, since it was 7:45 a.m. She turned left and ran down until she found a wide street called Blossom, then took another left and made her way back. She'd seen a Starbucks between the pub and the hotel the night before, and decided to stop for coffee. She bought water, ordered a vanilla latte and sat at a patio table, reading the newspaper. At 9:30, when the streets were noticeably busier she decided to go get ready for the day. The festivities started at ten, but the band wasn't performing until four in the afternoon. They were third on the line-up and the only thing they had to do was to take their instruments to the stage and do a quick sound check before the first band started at noon.

The shower was running when she walked into the room. She placed her newspaper on the night stand, took off her running shoes, and walked toward her bag on the floor. Kneeling in front of it, she started to rummage through her clothes.

When the door of the bathroom opened, John came out shirtless and damp, with his toiletry bag in one hand. He seemed as surprised to see her as she was to see him, even though he was in her room.

Startled by the sight of him, she stood up quickly and almost lost her footing due to lack of blood in her brain.

"Are you okay?" He lifted his hand and touched her arm with the tips of his fingers.

Thank goodness, she was pressing her forehead with her hand, thus shielding her eyes from him, because she couldn't look away from his chest. The prickly fuzz of black hair, and the hardness of his muscles adorned by droplets of water would be enough to make her crawl up the walls; add his erect nipples and the scent of his skin in the mix, and she was burning in places she couldn't name.

"Yeah. I thought you were Matt," she said, while thinking to herself 'Audrey, you really need to get laid'.

"Matt went to get aspirin. I was about to knock on Kevin and Tyler's door, and he said I could shower here to save time. I have to go talk to the festival's coordinator."

"Of course. You don't have to explain."

He walked past her toward the bed, and grabbed his T-shirt. As he was putting it on, he said, "I didn't want to look like I've just walked in here."

"John, you don't have to cater to me."

"Oh, I know."

"Sometimes I feel like, uh, an inconvenience to you."

"You're not... Do I make you feel like that?

Audrey nodded.

"I'm sorry. You don't inconvenience me at all, it's quite the contrary," he said, walking toward the door.

Quite the contrary? She thought.

"You've been great…Helpful." He seemed flustered, holding on the door knob for dear life. "I've got to go."

"Okay," she said, her voice as small as a toddler's.

*

If it wasn't for check-out at eleven a.m., none of the boys would had gotten up before late afternoon the next day. The Saint Patrick's Day festival had been great: the band sounded terrific, the people were friendly, and Guinness abounded. Tyler indeed had required privacy, but fortunately the girl took him to her house. It was the beauty of college towns: they functioned like a giant dorm.

Driving away from Columbia, they watched from the tour bus kids gliding on rubber tubes down the river that cut the city, scattered cars dotting the shoulders of the road, and men with fish rods standing on bridges. Since Kevin, Tyler, and Matt wouldn't stop complaining about their hangover, John agreed to stop. Rob steered off the narrow road that was taking them to the Congaree National Park, where they intended to camp for the night before heading to Georgia. He drove the Winnebago as far into the woods as he could as if trying to conceal it from the passing cars.

Uncertain of how long the boys intended to stay there, Audrey took a couple of the many books she'd bought in one of the city's used books store the day before. "That will be great." She tilted her head toward the cooler and the tequila bottle Tyler carried. "For when the State troopers stop to find out why a RV is parked on the side of the road."

"Now I know who the designated driver will be." He winked at her.

She looked for a spot in the sun to sit down. There weren't many smooth areas; tree roots punctured the water, and rocks and moss framed the river. Her only option was to walk up the bank and sit on a weedy patch of grass relatively far from the rest of them.

Kevin, Matt, and Tyler made a game of walking up- river several feet past a big rock near the other bank and floating down while trying to land on it, which proved rather difficult because of the strong current that pulled them away. From time to time, she glanced at them and at John who leaned against a tree drinking a beer. Under the warm sun, almost an hour went by, Kevin sat on the rock with a beer can in each hand. Matt, Tyler and John were talking near the water.

"Audrey let's get in the water. It's not too cold. You have to do it at least once for memory's sake," Matt shouted, startling her. She turned her face toward him and blocked the sun from her eyes with the book she was reading. The temperature was about fifty degrees, the sun felt warm, but there was still a cold bite in the air. No way the water wasn't freezing.

"John hasn't made any memories yet and I don't hear you asking him to get in the water."

John was fully dressed, sitting on the cooler, and holding a beer when Matt gave him a pleading look. John snorted, put down his can, and yanked off his boots.

"Yee-ha! It's on," Tyler said.

John stood and pulled his T-shirt over his head. Audrey propped herself on her elbows and inhaled deeply as his abdominal muscles expanded and the fabric, rubbing against his skin, revealed his bronzed shoulders and messed up his hair.

She wasn't sure if what bothered her was he looked so attractive or that he was getting into the cold water to make her get in. When he stripped to his boxers, she had to remember to breathe. "Snap out of it! He's not into you," her brain warned her.

Without ever looking at her he stepped into the water. "Fuck," he said, his skin raised in goosebumps.

Even from far, she could see his body hair glistening against the sunshine, making him glimmer like a deity. When the water reached his knees, he turned to face them and fell backwards until it covered his whole body. Simultaneously, Matt and Tyler turned to her.

"Go Audrey. You can do it." Kevin lifted his beer enthusiastically.

She placed her book on the ground. Okay, at least, you're gonna put down that fire. She was wearing a yellow tank top and cargo shorts. She could just get in the water dressed, but she hadn't brought a towel, and the thought of walking back to the bus soaking wet stifled her inhibitions. She unbuttoned her shorts; all eyes were on her. She gave Matt and Tyler an irked look, but focused her gaze on the water. She wobbled the shorts off her hips with her thumbs and it fell down her legs, revealing a purple leopard-print boy shorts-style panty. Then, she took her top off and adjusted the strap of the white bra that had fallen off her shoulder. Her eyes met John's before he turned away and waded toward Kevin.

Disappointed her stripping didn't seem to affect him as much as his had affected her, she walked casually toward the river. A wave of shock traveled through her body when she stepped into the water.

"I hate your guts," she shouted as the air escaped her lungs. After the initial shock, numbness replaced the pain. She and Matt stumbled up the river carefully diving forward where the water seemed deep enough—no more than her waist line, both laughing whenever there was a slip and the other lost their footing.

"My feet hurts." Matt turned around and floated his way down.

"Chicken." She continued walking, but suddenly shrieked in pain and tumbled in the water.

"What's wrong?" John said.

"Something on my foot," she said, surprised at having him right beside her. She'd been busy trying to stand and steady herself against the current, she hadn't noticed him coming to her aid. He must have darted from the rock to be by her side so quickly.

"Let me see, grab my shoulder." He leaned forward so she could put her hand on his shoulder and reached down.

"I'm going to pull your foot out of the water so I can take a look." A heartbeat passed, and he said, "You've got about a two-inch cut. I think you might even need stitches."

"That's a nasty cut." Matt was leaning forward, too, coming closer.

"Let's get you out of the water," John said.

Audrey wasn't expecting a 'Let's get you out of the water.' He said it so protectively she wasn't sure this was the same guy who had been ignoring her for nearly two weeks.

"Sounds good." She placed her other hand on Matt's shoulder, and they carried her out of the water.

She sat on a tree root while John knelt in front of her. He placed her foot on his leg. If it wasn't for the pain shooting up her leg, she would have thought she was blushing for having him so close.

"Grab my shirt, Matt, will ya?" He pointed down the riverbank.

"How bad is it?" Audrey asked.

"Definitely needs stitches…Hang on." He squeezed her ankle and pressed his fingers into the cut.

Feeling the pain, she reflexively tried to pull her foot away, but he held her ankle and he pulled a green piece of glass from the cut.

"Looks like it's from a beer bottle. Heineken."

"Yuck, I hate Heineken." She gave the faintest smile and he responded with a small chuckle, a surprising sign of laughter completely foreign to her.

"At least, it's not rusted metal," Matt said, arriving with the T-shirt.

"Wait . . ." she said as John swaddled it around her foot. "Don't get your shirt"—she muttered in defeat—"dirty."

This time, John smiled at her.

"I guess we will have to leave now, huh?" Kevin said approaching them.

"I'm sorry to disturb you, your highness," she said, bowing her head.

"We have to take you to a hospital." John stood and offered his hand.

"I'll grab our stuff." Rob turned away followed by Tyler.

John helped her up and, in a quick motion, drew one hand behind her back, the other around her knees, and lifted her on his arms.

"Whoa, John." Audrey threw her arm around his shoulder. "This way both of us will get hurt."

"You shouldn't put pressure on that foot, it might worsen the bleeding." He walked up the bank with little effort.

"Thank you," she said softly.

"You're welcome." He looked into her eyes.

She felt her cheeks blotch but she wasn't about to complain. For one; he was actually talking to her, and two; she was in his arms, against his bare chest, feeling it expand with the quickening of his breathing as he carried her to the bus.

*

After she filled out the admission form, the nurses assessed the situation of her foot and sent her back to the waiting room to wait for a doctor. John waited with her, while everyone else went to a grocery store they'd driven by on their way to the hospital.

"We need supplies," Kevin had said, which literally translated to alcohol and cookies.

She sat beside John, not knowing what to say. She wished Matt had stayed as well; he would fill the silence with his usual chitchat, but she hadn't asked. It wasn't like her to ask people for anything.

"I hope I haven't bled out completely by the time they're ready to stitch me up." Audrey regretted her attempt at small talk as soon as the words came out. She wasn't bleeding very much, and the new bandage the nurse dressed her foot with was almost clean.

"More likely, you'll die of infection by then."

"I appreciate you waiting with me. You didn't have to."

"I'm going to see it to the end." John gave her a sideway glance. "You handled yourself pretty well in an emergency."

"Thanks. I have two younger brothers."

"I have to say, your help—although greatly appreciated—was most unexpected."

"Oh." He looked down at his feet.

"I'm sorry I don't mean to nag, I thought, uh—" She wasn't sure she should go down that path. "I mean, you haven't seemed to particularly care much for me."

"You don't have to apologize, I know I haven't been exactly friendly, I just don't . . . converse well with new people," he said, blushing.

"We've been inside the Winnebago for two weeks."

"I know, but you're a girl. A pretty girl." He rubbed his boots together, face turning purple and looking as if he was about to hide behind a chair.

"Are you telling me you're shy?"

"Some people call it that."

"But you're in a band. On a stage. In front of heaps of people."

"That's different. On stage I'm performing, you know? Just doing my job. Besides I'm more focused on the music than the audience."

She nodded, staring at nothing as if the invisible pieces of a puzzle were coming together in front of her.

"And I close my eyes a lot." John smiled at her.

"Hmm, yes, you do," she said, smiling back.

She had never pictured him as a shy person; if anything, he appeared self-assured and proud—a snob. He didn't try to prove himself or to take part in a conversation as shy people sometimes feel compelled to. On the contrary, he detached himself from attention, but the band swarmed around him like bees in honeysuckle.

After John's confession, they eased into conversation, and when the nurse called out her name, they were twenty minutes into talking about their childhood cuts and scrapes.

"See? Still alive," John said.

Audrey smiled and hobbled toward the nurse, who held a large wood door open.

Halfway there, she turned to John. "Will you come with me?"

*

"Can you believe how gratuitously doctors prescribe antibiotics these days?" She waved the prescription in the air, lying on the Winnebago's couch while they drove to Augusta. The drive back to a hospital in Columbia had altered their plans to camp for the night.

"I know, isn't it great?" Kevin said, sitting at the table with Matt. Tyler drove. Rob and John sat on the bed in the back.

"Great, if you want to raise an army of pharmacologically induced zombies," she said.

"Ah, soldier, you may be on to something now."

Audrey looked at Kevin, ticked off.

"It's America," Matt added.

"You know, now that I'm thinking about it, I remember my father coming back from Brazil with at least a few boxes of amoxicillin. I think you don't need prescriptions there if you know what to ask for."

"Are you going to fill your prescription?" Matt asked.

"Not sure yet. The doctor said I should start taking the antibiotics in case it gets infected, but if it never does, I still have to take the pills for ten days to finish the treatment."

"Just wait and see, then," Matt said.

"But if you wait and it becomes something worse, you might have complications. Besides, we might be in the middle of nowhere, and you'd have to wait to go back to a doctor. You should take it." John stood and leaned against the door.

She considered what he said for a moment. "I'm going to wait. I'm like my mother; I hate taking medicine."

Without replying, he walked to the front and sat on the passenger seat by Tyler.

"Okay, so your mother—who is from the drugs-for-all country—hates taking medicine? That's ironic," Kevin said.

"Those drugs still cost a lot of money. Some people still have to rely on popular wisdom and herbs to get better." Audrey put her earbuds in and turned her head away.

Chapter 7

The night in Augusta was a chilly one. She wanted to crank up the heater in her room but couldn't make herself get out of bed. An erratic tug on her foot kept her awake, she propped it on top of two pillows and lay on her side in almost a fetal position, with her thumb pressing her lips. Why wasn't Tylenol helping? Usually two pills were enough to make her relax. She never had insomnia and, after the day she had, it was unbelievable her dissolute mind wouldn't give in to her body's exhaustion.

She made an effort not to think at all and only contemplate the supple shapes created on the sheer drapes by the shadows outside. They morphed and merged on the fabric that danced to the rumbling air coming from the air-conditioning unit right below the window. A silhouette walked by, engulfing the tiny shadows in darkness like a towering giant. She stretched her neck like a flamingo and rested on her elbows. The stream of light coming from under the door was blocked by whoever stood in front of it, then moved in the direction it came from.

"Hello?" She shouted before the shadow could disappear into the opaque wall.

Gone. She flopped down into the bed, hating herself for hesitating.

"Audrey, are you awake?" John's voice came from the door. "I brought you water."

Audrey hopped her way to the door. John had two bottles of water and a Snickers bar in his hands.

"What time is it?" She asked.

"Not sure. About one, I think." He handed her one of the bottles and the candy bar but didn't move, like a vampire waiting for an invitation.

"Thanks. Stay a while if you're not too tired."

He stepped inside and closed the door.

She unwrapped the chocolate and took a big bite. "I think this is what has been keeping me awake all night. There is nothing like a midnight snack." Her mouth overflowed with chocolate and she lifted a hand to cover it up. John chuckled and, for a moment, she was caught up in his smile.

Oh, wow. She let out a breath she didn't realize she was holding.

Something had just changed; amorphous feelings started to take shape. It was that split second in someone's life when love becomes tangible even if not recognized or understood. Her heart skipped a beat, but she didn't act under any illusions on that account. Instead, she hopped back to her bed and John lay down on the other one. They stared at the ceiling and, for a few minutes, the only noise in the room was the humming of the decrepit air conditioning unit.

"What were you guys doing?" Audrey finally asked.

"Nothing. We were hanging out in the bus. Tyler was trying to come up with an alternative for Red Bull and vodka using Mello Yello from the vending machine and tequila."

"Really? And?"

"Not good. Now we're out of tequila. We had to do shots to wash out the bad taste."

"Don't you ever get tired of being on that bus?"

"Not yet, I guess. I've been waiting for a long time for this."

"I see." She sat up on the bed, opened her water bottle, and drank half of it with large gulps. "Have you ever thought about doing something else?" She wiped her mouth with her arm.

"Nothing that isn't related to music. I said to myself: if in five years with the band I can't make a living, I'll find another way."

"How long has it been?"

"Five years."

"I'm glad it's working out." She reached for the pillows at the end of the bed and propped them in position again.

"Need a hand?"

46

"Nah, I got it." She placed her foot on the pillows and lay down, grimacing with discomfort.

"You really should take the antibiotics," he said, but she responded only with a faint smile. "How about you? Have you thought of doing something else besides photography?"

Audrey snorted, not used to being referred to as a photographer. "I've thought about doing a million things, from being a fashion designer to working with indigenous tribes in the Amazon. I guess I get that from my mother. She was always restless, pursuing several things at once but never sticking to one long enough to see results. So she was, mostly, a stay-at-home mom with big dreams."

He was staring at her. Disconcerted, she returned her gaze to the ceiling and said, "Growing up, I was her business partner." Audrey smiled. "She told me about the value of work and how it can dignify even the most hopeless of souls. She never accepted just being at home, even when my father had told her he could take care of us and she shouldn't worry about it. It wasn't about money for her, which was good, because she never made any. I remember once she decided to make homemade truffles and chocolate-covered candy. Bombons, as they call it in Brazil. She went out and spent over two hundred dollars in tools and supplies, but sold only sixty dollars worth of chocolate. My father and I ate truffles for weeks."

"I wouldn't mind that."

"Oh, I didn't. Not at all. Except for seeing her face afterwards. She never said anything but I could see the disappointment in her eyes."

The noise from the air conditioner took over the room again as they lapsed into silence.

"You still haven't told me what you wanted to do."

"I . . . ." She let out a sigh and offered him a vague smile. She could have told him she wanted to be a photographer, but she knew it wasn't the truth. She still didn't know what she wanted.

She knew she didn't want to spend years doing a job she hated or marry a boyfriend she didn't love, and most certainly, she didn't want to stumble through life anymore.

Chapter 8

Photographing the band with an injured foot had proved more challenging than she'd anticipated. After one week, she finally removed the stitches in a Minute Clinic on their way to Tuscaloosa, where the band was going to have the last gig on Saturday before heading out to Texas. She still felt a pinch of pain at every step, but she didn't hesitate to walk normally anyway, afraid her leg would atrophy from lack of use. It was an absurd fear, but it had been subconsciously imprinted on her mind from knowing a beloved aunt wasted away to her death after becoming paraplegic in a car accident in Brazil.

Over the past few days, John's animosity had transformed into something else. He still stood away, towering over everyone like a centenary oak tree when Kevin and Tyler were showing off or competing for her attention. But now she could escape the noise and join him in his quietness. He no longer fled.

They had arrived in Tuscaloosa on Wednesday, and the next day she woke early to survey the town and work on her own photography. After her conversation with John, she'd decided photography was no longer going to be only an avocation. The early hours of the morning had its advantages: the light was beautiful and she could be alone. Completely alone.

"I was looking for you." John was sitting on the stairs that led up to the second floor of the hotel, when she got back at eleven.

"I was photographing some places around town." She wasn't sure what her professional inclinations were yet, but nature wasn't her forte. Not because she didn't like it or appreciate its beauty, but because anything short of Edward Weston was not even worth pursuing. Perfectionism and indecisiveness had proven to be a bad combo. She was drawn to people, everything about the human presence intrigued her. Even when determined to photograph the historic centers of the little towns they drove through, she'd find herself taking pictures of graffiti on building walls, interesting bystanders, or pie displays inside run-down diners.

"Cool. Anything good?"

"Oh, the usual. I'm still looking for...inspiration." She felt embarrassed about the truth. She walked around with her D90 furtively pressing the shutter at the things she saw, but she ached for meaning—for her images, for her life.

"It will come to you." John nodded as if he understood the subtext. "Listen, I found out about this little museum they have here. It's called the Westervelt, and it's supposedly huge on American Art. Do you want to go check it out?"

She was caught off guard. It was the first time he'd asked her to do anything. "Yeah, sure."

"It opens at noon. We can take a cab."

"Okay."

They rode in silence to the Westervelt. The drive was scenic and calm, but her mind was racing. Unable to decode her thoughts into a coherent explanation, she overheated like an overloaded CPU.

The museum was a beautiful stone mansion that sat on a hill surrounded by trees. Inside, the surroundings were as warm and rich as a log cabin, with high ceilings and walnut paneled walls. Works of art were spread all over rooms which resembled more a large house than a museum.

"Look, Durand's *Progress*." John pointed to a large landscape painting with a baroque gold frame hanging on a corner.

"Wow." Audrey approached the painting. It was breathtaking, with its vast lavender sky, bathed in golden rays of sun that seemed to emanate out of the canvas. "How did you know?"

"I've taken some art classes."

"Did you?" Her voice was soft, wavering between incredulity and joy.

"I thought they went well with my music major." He glanced at her, then returned his gaze to the painting. "Durant said, 'Let the artist scrupulously accept whatever nature presents him until he shall, in a degree, have become intimate with her infinity.' I tend to think of nature as life." He smiled at her and walked to the next painting.

"How did you start with music?"

"My mother. She died when I was younger."

"I'm sorry."

"It's okay, It was a long time ago. She loved music. She played several instruments. She gave me my acoustic guitar."

"The one—" Audrey lifted a finger over her shoulder and gestured toward the direction they'd come from.

"Yes. I always have it with me."

"Aw," she murmured. It was the saddest, sweetest thing she'd ever heard. Staring at him surveying the art, she bit her lower lip and braced herself to fight the urge to step closer and hug him.

*

"Audrey? Earth to Audrey. . . ." Matt's voice sounded distant, even though he was sitting next to her at the pub. "Is everything okay?" He asked when she looked at him.

"Yes. Why?"

"I don't know. You look worried."

"I'm okay." She grasped the back of her hair with both hands and twisted it in a makeshift pony tail, letting its long strands fall over her right shoulder.

This cannot be happening to me. She squeezed her beer bottle and pretended not to watch John at the bar talking to the pub owner.

When Audrey and John had arrived back from the museum in the afternoon, Matt, Tyler, and Kevin were throwing a football in the hotel parking lot. They all played for a while, but Audrey wanted to be alone. Her head had been spinning ever since the incident in Columbia. She was glad John had finally stopped avoiding her, but now she felt her insides melt when he was near. It was nauseating.

"Where's Rob?" John said.

"He took the bus to the mechanic," Matt said.

It was ironic how they always referred to the decrepit Winnebago as the bus, for tour bus.

"Where have you two been?" Kevin threw the ball to Audrey.

"At a museum." She caught it without difficulty.

"Nice catch," Tyler said.

"My father wanted a son." She threw the ball at Tyler in a perfect spiral.

When they knocked on her room door and invited her to go hang out at the pub where they were going to perform the next day, she almost said no, but figured staying alone ruminating on her feelings was worse. She needed distraction.

"From Gary." A waiter placed Jägermeister shots on the table. They looked over at the bar and Gary, the pub owner, waved at them. They'd met him the night before, the first time they went to the pub to introduce themselves and check out the place. After the high-tech company Gary had worked for went under, he bought the bar and moved from Silicon Valley to run it.

"I think he's interested," Tyler smirked.

Audrey lifted her glass, nodded at Gary, and dropped her head, feeling the burning in her throat and the heat crawling up her chest. It was exactly what she needed to forget what was happening to her. Happened to her. Stupid Penny Lane. She gulped the rest of her beer. Stupid. Stupid. Stupid.

"Wanna dance?" She asked Matt.

"Dance?" He stiffened.

"I'll go with you." Kevin quickly offered. Audrey glanced at Kevin, then back at Matt.

"Go. I'll take the next one," Matt smiled shyly.

Audrey shrugged. "Come on, Kevin." They walked toward the

empty dance floor—a small area in front of the tiny stage.

The band performing had an upbeat sound that reminded her of Maroon 5. The lead singer let out a little cheer when he saw them approaching, moving with the beat of the drums. The music transformed her body into a malleable material that bended and flailed, as sinuously as a dangerous road. She raised her arms and Kevin placed his hands on her waist. For a moment, she had the urge to look at the bar to see if John was watching, but he wasn't there. Gary, though, was behind the bar and couldn't take his eyes off her. She looked at the table where she'd come from, John was sitting with the guys. His name vibrated in her head along with the stirring music. John, John, John. She threw herself into it and danced until her hair felt heavy and damp, clinging to her back and neck. When the music stopped, Kevin gave her a celebratory hug and led her toward the table.

"I'm going to get something to drink." She veered toward the bar.

The reality was, she didn't want to be in John's vicinity just yet. Her last relationship had ended very badly and, in the two years she'd spent with that boyfriend, she had not once felt the throbbing of wild horses crushing her chest like she did when John was around. Strangely enough, she also experienced an incredible serenity, as if she was riding up a mountain in a ski-lift, watching the smooth white carpet below her while cool snowflakes flickered and melted on her face.

"What can I get you, gorgeous?" Gary placed a napkin in front of her.

"Jack and water." Audrey sat on a vacant stool at the edge of the bar and he turned to mix it. He placed the drink in front of her, and she pulled a twenty from her pocket.

"No, on the house." Gary dismissed the money with a wave of his hand.

"Thanks." Audrey knew there was no point on insisting. Every other round the band consumed was on the house. Gary wouldn't allow her to pay, considering his obvious interest. She felt a pang of devilish shame about the situation, because his tanned Californian looks didn't do anything for her. Even if the thoughts of John weren't constantly pulsing in her head, like the first signs of a massive migraine, Gary's 'what's-up-dude' attitude appeared to be that of someone trying very hard to live in a decade that had long bid farewell.

"You looked pretty good on the dance floor," Gary said.

"Oh." Audrey wasn't sure how to respond to being complimented on something as frivolous as dancing. She hadn't somersaulted backwards, for goodness sake. "Thanks." While she couldn't think of a single reason to stay there and endure Gary's foundering attempts to charm her, sitting by John was not a better prospect. She wanted to. Oh, hell. She wanted it to be near him so bad, she'd started to daydream about it, but being unemployed, living with her parents, and absolutely clueless as to what to do with her life kept any hopes of a relationship at bay.

"Come sit with us." Matt leaned on the bar. "Can I have four Budweisers, please?" He asked a young bartender. Gary was at the opposite side of the bar talking to other patrons.

"Matt, have you ever been afraid?" Audrey said, without looking at him.

"What have you been drinking?" Matt reached for her glass, and sniffed the liquid inside it.

"When you started the band. How did you know you were going to get along?"

"Well, I didn't start the band. John did. I just joined in. I didn't know if we were going to get along and we didn't—all the time, he kept us together."

"Hmm," Audrey took a sip of her whiskey and pondered. "Weren't you worried John wasn't going to reciprocate your... efforts?" Audrey bit her lower lip, wishing she could stuff those words back into her mouth, because Matt's expression was torn between amusement and incredulity.

There was a moment of silence, long enough for Audrey to knock back her drink and wish to burst in flames.

Matt's expression turned contemplative, then he said, "I suppose we never know what other people will do, that's why we can't worry about it. What we can do is not let fear keep us from living the best life we can." He paid for the beer the bartender had placed in front of him, then intertwined his long fingers on the bottles, two in each hand. "I can tell you one thing for sure, John is the best person to share your *efforts* with, because he always does what's in his power not to let anyone down."

Chapter 9

"Want to go on a hike?" Matt asked John, as he and Audrey stepped on the curb and made their way to the hill behind their hotel the next day. They ran almost daily, before they got in the bus or after getting out. No matter when, Matt was the one who insisted on running, he had explained he was built like Jon Favreau, always on the line between fit and fat. Audrey didn't mind. She pushed herself to exhaustion, so she could fall into bed and be unconscious before a veil of troubled thoughts covered her like a wet blanket.

"Nah." John regarded them with mild attention, sitting under a tree on the curb beside the bus with his guitar cradled on his lap.

"Are you working on a new song?" Audrey thought she'd seen a flicker in John's eyes when he looked at her and felt her cheeks heat up. Oh, hell. She wanted to pinch those little traitors.

"You can say that."

As they started their hike, Matt told her the band had hundreds of songs composed by John. However, not all having earned his approval, he continued to work on them endlessly.

Matt and Audrey hiked hard; embarrassment can be a huge motivator, she discovered. Usually, she and Matt talked quite a bit, but she dreaded he was going to ask her about their conversation at the bar the night before, so she kept a steady pace. She didn't have any excuse to give him besides being drunk, which Matt wouldn't accept easily. He'd seen her drink much more without losing her composure. She could handle her alcohol and he knew it.

"Am I being punished for something?" He asked, bending over with his hands on his knees.

Turning back to look at him, she couldn't help but laugh. "What's the matter Charlie Brown? Don't think you can make it?"

"If I had known today was boot-camp day, I would still be in bed."

"Oh, come on. No pain, no gain, remember?"

Matt's flushed face and ragged breathing told her words of encouragement wouldn't work. Obviously, he didn't have any troubling thoughts to distract him from the exertion.

"Let's head back." She marched down the trail and patted his back as he gave her a grateful smile.

Nearing John again, still sitting in the same position as they had left him, she bit her lips and took in the view. The very sight of him wreaked a havoc of emotions inside her; she could barely recognize herself.

"How is it coming?" Matt asked John. "Do you need an audience?" He teased, but John responded with a contemptuous look.

John and Matt were the two people she didn't need to be around. The last thing she wanted was John to find out about her feelings through a petty attempt to undermine a joke or smart-ass remark Matt could make.

"Okay, then. I'm off to town, I need some things." Audrey walked away, feeling Matt's and John's eyes on her back.

When she came back later in the afternoon, the guys were watching TV in the hotel room that was transformed in the band's headquarters. So far, only Kevin, Matt, and Tyler had slept in it, but they'd all used the shower. How they got the clerk to agree to such arrangement was beyond her grasp, but she had gotten her own room. It was all she needed to know.

There was some reality show marathon on TV and the boys laughed and criticized at the same time.

"Are you going out for dinner tonight?" Audrey asked, looking at the TV and flinching at the image of a girl wearing hot pink tongues sticking out from a pair of low-rise jeans.

"Forget it," Kevin said.

"No way, we've ordered pizza," Matt said.

"Snooki is about to get in the hot tub." Tyler said, and Rob nodded.

She crossed the room toward the bottle of tequila over a corner table and poured herself a shot. John sat on one of the chairs with his heels propped on the table.

"Do you want to have dinner? I've got to have a real meal." Audrey circled her finger around the rim of the glass.

"Sure." If he was surprised by her invitation, he didn't show it.

"In one hour, then." She swigged the tequila, wincing at the burn.

As she walked in front of the TV, Kevin grabbed her by the waist. "Let's watch Jersey Shore together. We need a female's point of view."

She freed herself and squeezed his nose, saying, "over my dead body," and pushed him onto the bed.

In her room, she laid the dress perfectly flat on the bed, pale pink with tiny black flowers and vines that from the distance looked like spider webs. It had been weeks since she had worn a dress. Jeans and casual tops had been her uniform—the appropriate wardrobe when you hang around a bunch of guys you're not trying to impress. That night was different because she wanted to impress a guy. Thinking about him had become a torture, with heat scorching her skin every time he walked by. She had given it a lot of thought and had come up with three likely outcomes for the night; one—he would refuse her, she would be utterly embarrassed, and would have to get over him and move on; two—they would sleep together but he wouldn't want anything beyond that, so she would have to get over him and move on; and three—he would reciprocate her feelings and they would make incandescent love all night. She knew in all of those scenarios, there was still a potential hiccup—the band. Leaving them mid-tour because of an affair gone sour was an outcome she didn't want to consider.

In the shower, she tried to remember if she had ever been this nervous about going out with a man. Since the night John had fallen asleep in her room in Augusta she couldn't think about anything else. She closed her eyes and remembered his arms around her, carrying her to the bus when she cut her foot. She could feel electricity between them, but he'd never made a move.

Perhaps the amounts of testosterone and tequila inside the tour bus clouded her perception—Kevin, Matt, and Tyler acted like the Three Stooges. Rob was reserved and focused on doing his job. And John? John was untroubled, serious, and kind. There seemed to be a universe inside him where he got everything he needed—the wisdom and contentment people spent their entire lives searching for.

She fought off a sudden wave of dizziness, but it was too late to bail. So, the least she could do was to bring out her guns, which meant buttering up with lotion, lacy panties—the uncomfortable kind—and smokey eyes. She slipped on the dress and put on her boots, and styled her long brown hair to accentuate its natural curls, put a dab of lip balm on her lips and a drop of perfume behind her earlobes. She blushed at her reflection in the mirror.

*

Exactly one hour had passed when she pushed the door open and walked into the room. All gazes fell on her, but she played it down.

"So?" She twirled around.

Silence.

"Wow!" Tyler finally said.

John had changed his shirt and by the smell of soap and damp hair, she assumed he had managed to take a shower. The tequila bottle was almost empty, and the pizza had been reduced to crumbs inside its open box. She hoped he hadn't eaten any of it; despite everything else, she was hungry.

"Let's go," she urged him.

They had to walk less than ten minutes to get to the restaurant. They were staying at a motel off the highway and, since driving the tour bus to anywhere was too much of a hassle, the best they could do under the circumstances was a Macaroni Grill across the street.

"This should be fun," she said.

"What?"

"Having a grown-up meal, just the two of us."

"Are you serious? Who is the grown up here?"

Stop over-thinking.

After all, it was John. They'd spent time together, they knew each other. Yet she felt a cloud of ambiguity hovering over them and John must had felt it as well, because he decided to blow it over before it became a storm.

He held her arm to make her stop before they walked up the steps to the restaurant, and said, "Audrey, just so we're clear..."

Oh, God. He is putting me in my place right now.

"Are you looking for an excuse to wear your new dress or... what is this?"

"John..." Only, what to say? I think you're cool and I was hoping to get laid tonight. If true, it could work with any other of the guys, but not with John. She didn't know what this was, she suspected was more than sex, otherwise sleeping with Kevin or Tyler would—

Before she found the words to answer his question, he leaned forward and kissed her. His hands held the small of her back and pulled her close. Her heart punched in her chest, as if an alien was trying to rip her ribcage open. She placed her arms around his neck and kissed him back. The smell of his skin, the warmth of his lips, and the taste of his tongue was intoxicating. She wanted to undress him right there, but instead she summoned the strength to say, "Let's eat," and with a hand on his chest, pushed herself gently out of his arms.

He gave her the same smile she'd seen only once. It made her feel like a tiny leaf that, tossed by the wind, had traveled the world to come to that spot, at that instant, to witness that smile. One thing she'd learned about John and could not take for granted: he didn't open himself frivolously to everyone. At that moment, he was opening himself to her in his smile. She let out the slightest sigh of satisfaction as he touched her forehead with his. It seemed they had shared the same fears and the same desires all along and, as the realization dawned on her, she laughed out loud; and so did he.

Gesso arches were stenciled with vines not burdened by the weight of the full and round grape bunches painted on them. A short line of burgundy-colored upholstered booths were dimly lit by low-hanging lamps above the tables and votive candles inside stained glass holders. The porcelain-faced hostess led them to the last booth, handed out the menus, and left with the same enthusiasm of a funerary home attendant.

"Not sure about the food, but her enthusiasm is contagious." Audrey looked at him mockingly.

"That's the beauty of chain restaurants, If you've been to one, you already know what to expect—at least from the food."

When the waitress came over bearing two glasses of water, John ordered a Chianti from the wine list.

Audrey looked over the menu, but the only thing she could think about was the interrupted kiss in the parking lot. She should have taken him back to her room and ordered pizza, now she had to sit across the table and make casual conversation. How could she feel she knew everything that was to know about him, when in reality she knew nothing at all? A musician, older sibling, deceased mother, incredibly kind and attentive. Shy. Sexy. Soft lips.

"Tell me about your family." John lifted his glass and took a sip of wine. As always, if he was nervous, she couldn't tell. The waitress reappeared and they ordered: fettuccine alfredo for him and four cheese ravioli for her.

"I'm the only child. My mother is Brazilian, and she met my dad when she came to the U.S. to work as a caregiver to an elderly gentleman whose daughter was too busy to do it herself."

"Have you been to Brazil?" The waitress sat their salads in front of them.

"Yes, many times. My family used to spend summers there. Well, my father couldn't stay more than two weeks because of his job. But after he returned to the U.S., my mother and I would spend the rest of vacation living like typical Brazilians at my grandparent's farm in the middle of the country."

"A farm, really?"

"Yes, that's where my mom grew-up. My grandparents still live there."

"What did you do on a farm for a whole summer?"

"Lots of things. I've helped my grandfather milk the cows, ride horses, swim in the river, cook with my grandmother on a wood-stove."

"That's neat."

"It was. I have cousins my age, so we played around mango trees all day. When we were hungry, we could just pluck a mango off the tree and eat it."

"Cool."

"Actually, they are in peak in November, when twenty-eight mango trees make the air around the farmhouse fragrant and sweet. I'd pull their skin with my teeth and bite their stringy yellow flesh until I hit the pit. I'd eat so many my gums hurt afterwards." Audrey said longingly.

"Do you speak Portuguese?" John ferried salad to his mouth with fervor. She guessed he was more relaxed—or nervous—than usual, because she'd never seen him eat like that.

"I think I still do," she pondered. "I haven't been to Brazil in ten years."

"How come? It sounded like you loved it there."

Suddenly, she was uncomfortable. "My mother started to talk about moving down there for good. My father didn't want to."

She looked at the table and took a sip of wine. "I grew up and got tired of, um, ah, having to reacquaint myself every summer to the place, the people…I guess—"

"Say something in Portuguese." John's voice was more cheery, and she felt a rush of gratitude for his intervention.

"*Demorei uma eternidade para chegar aqui.*" Audrey's lips twitched upwards in a tiny smile.

"What does it mean?"

"It took me forever to get here." She bit her lower lip.

"I know what you mean." John's eyes were eager, conspiratorial.

*

On the walk back to the hotel he reached for her hand, lacing his fingers with hers and smiling shyly.

"I want to show you something." She led him up the same hill she hiked earlier with Matt.

After five minutes, they veered off the trail into a clearing where a patch of grass seemed to thrive. They could see the Winnebago parked sideways in the empty motel parking lot and the town's scant skyline.

"This view is amazing," John said.

Yellow lights twinkled in the distance, probably little farm houses not pushed out by urbanization, with bare trees outlined by the moonlight.

"I knew it was going to look great under the moon, a perfect picture of an American small town, like in a vintage postcard." She sat on the grass and he sat beside her, admiring the view in silence for a while.

He lay down and put his arm out; she rested her head on his chest and they watched the sky. His heart pounded inside his chest as fast as hers and in perfect harmony.

"When I was a kid camping with my parents, sometimes in the back yard, I used to trace the stars. Not to find constellations, but to create whatever shape I wanted." Even as an adult, she couldn't recognize any constellations, except by the obvious Big Dipper.

John murmured under his breath, "When I trace the stars I see you." He was holding a strand of her hair. "That's a good line."

"Yes, it is." She hooked her leg on his and rolled over him, adjusting herself and feeling the bulge growing in his pants as she gently rocked on top of him. It made her tremble with excitement.

They resumed the kiss from the restaurant: sweet and tender in the beginning, but quickly becoming hot and deep as raw desire took over their senses. Under her dress, his hands trailed up her legs, strong and wanting. He sat up with her on his lap, and nibbled at her earlobe and the soft part of her slender neck. Audrey lifted her hands and, untying the knot of her halter dress, pulled it down. John held her gaze, pulled her closer, and kissed her collarbone. She arched her back and closed her eyes as he fondled her breasts and sucked ever so tenderly on her nipples.

He took his button-down shirt off and threw it on the ground beside them, maneuvering her on top of it. Then, he ripped off his T-shirt and, matching her smile, helped her out of her dress. She reached out, rubbed her hand between his legs, and unbuckled his belt. They were completely enthralled as they made love while staring deeply into each other's eyes.

"I love you," she whispered in his ear, thinking these words she'd considered so loaded came rushing to her mouth with such a power she had no strength to stop them.

"I love you, too," he said instantaneously. She stopped kissing him for a moment, afraid he responded too quickly, without thinking about what he had just said. Although she hadn't labeled it love until then, she'd lost sleep over it countless nights and didn't want him to take it lightly.

She looked into his eyes and said, "I want to make sure you understand . . . I love the band, I love the music, I love the road, but I *love* you."

"And I love you, Audrey. From the moment I saw you."

There was something about the way he looked at her. Perhaps a recognition, a realization, but it was as if she'd been balancing on a ball her whole life and now—for the first time—she was stepping on firm ground.

*

The moon had changed sides in the sky when they walked back to the hotel. The Jersey Shore marathon was over. Kevin and Matt were stretched on the beds and Tyler was sitting by the table. Rob was already asleep in the bus. On the television, she saw the black-and-white image of a woman on a pay phone, *The Twilight Zone*. Kevin and Tyler were smoking cigars and all three of them held plastic cups with Jack Daniel's and ice. Very fitting, she thought standing by the door holding hands with John in silence, and waiting for everyone's assessment. She didn't know if was the silence or the holding of hands that did the trick, but she knew by the look on their faces they understood what was happening.

In a cinematic way, Kevin slowly pointed his index finger at the two of them. "Oh, oh, oh! What did you guys do?" His face twisted, as if suddenly the channel had been changed to a comedy show. Then, he burst into getting-laid jokes, followed by Matt and Tyler.

Audrey's brows snapped together as she looked at John, who shrugged dismissively. Letting go of his hand, she walked toward the table, lifted the empty tequila bottle, and said, "No more tequila? You bastards."

Chapter 10

It was noon when Audrey and John sat at the diner by the hotel to have breakfast. She was feeling something akin to elation for being with him for almost twenty-four hours consecutively. They'd made love again and again in her room, then spooned in bed until they fell asleep exhausted and happy.

The rest of the band trickled in one by one, each looking more hung over than the last. They laughed and made bets on how bad the next to walk through the door would look. Kevin, as usual, was the last to show up, looking pale with blood-shot eyes. It was the night of their gig, so breakfast had to be extra hearty.

"What's the plan today?" Matt craned a gigantic piece of ham and cheese omelet to his mouth.

"The bar opens at five, but we don't go on until eight," John said.

"Awesome. I'm going back to bed." Kevin ran his fingers through his hair and tilted his head lazily backwards.

"I want to get there around six, though." John gave Kevin a reprimanding glance. "I hope we can sell some CDs this time." At the last gig, Kevin gave away more than half of the CDs the band had set aside to sell.

"If you guys aren't going anywhere for awhile, I'm going to take the bus back to the shop. I still hear a noise after they've replaced the break pads." Rob sipped his coffee.

"Can you give me a ride? Gary asked if I could take pictures of the bar for their website. I'm going to meet him there before it opens," Audrey said.

Matt, Tyler, and Kevin immediately turned their faces to John.

"What?" Audrey noticed their sardonic looks.

"He wants his easy-rider ass alone with you," Kevin blurted.

"Don't be a jerk." She placed her coffee cup on the table. Of course, she'd noticed Gary's interest as soon as he set his eyes on her, but she would rather eat cockroaches before letting Kevin's cynical comment get to her.

"Ha! He's going to have a sweet surprise tonight." Kevin spoke with his mouth full of pancakes.

"John beat him to the punch," Tyler said.

Under the table, John and Audrey had their pinky fingers crossed, but she knew better than to give them more ammunition.

"Rob, are you ready?" Audrey said, and John stood to let her out of the booth.

She squeezed by him and whispered, "See you later?" Very aware of the watchful eyes on them.

"Yes," he whispered back.

*

It was hard to photograph the concert while being completely hypnotized by John. She saw him on stage in a new light, the way he moved, the way he held the guitar and closed his eyes when he soloed. Images of the night before flashed through her eyes, blinding her with desire—his hands trailing over her body, followed by his mouth. Her skin felt like rice paper, barely containing her body from exploding and scattering into the air.

Satisfied with the photographs she'd taken, she sat at the bar.

Gary placed a beer in front of her and, nodding to the stage, said "They are really good."

"I know." She glanced at Gary and at the beer. "Thanks."

"Do you think they'd stay and play tomorrow, too?"

"I'm not sure. They have other concerts in Texas."

"Hmm." Gary seemed disappointed.

She only gave him a sideway glance, trying to keep her attention at the stage to defer conversation; otherwise, she feared he might make a pass at her. Their afternoon together had been more like an ambush date, after she photographed the bar, he offered to take her to the hotel. It was bad enough she had to hold on to him while riding his motorcycle through town, he stopped on the way and insisted in buying her coffee. When they finally arrived at the hotel, she jumped off and said goodbye while already walking away.

"Hey." Gary leaned against the inside of the bar, pondering. "Do you want to go somewhere later?" He cleared his throat. "Just us."

"Oh." Audrey feigned surprise. "Gary, I'm really flattered…but I am with"—she nodded toward the stage—"the band."

Gary turned his head. John was staring at her.

"Lucky man." He straightened himself up and tapped his fingers on the bar. Timely, someone two seats down ordered a beer and Gary left to tend to the customer.

She continued looking at John, who gave her a faint smile before returning his concentration to the performance.

After they played the encore, Kevin asked for everyone's attention. He'd never done that before, so she turned on the stool to face the stage. He announced a special treat was about to commence. John walked to the microphone with his acoustic guitar.

"This is a brand new song, something I've been working on," he said, looking at her. "So be kind to me."

He poured his heart out in the most beautiful song. If for everyone else this was just another love song, for her it was as if he was talking to her, singing about the feelings he'd confessed having for her the night before. A few people in the crowd followed his gaze and found her, standing now, with an astonished smile on her face. Someone shouted, "Oh, yes!" Her heart skipped a beat when he hit a chorus singing, "when I trace the stars all I see is your face," and "it's all I need to guide me through the darkness."

She didn't know he could sing, much less had such a voice—raspy and deep. When the song was over, he put his guitar down and strode toward her. The room erupted in noise as he made his way through the crowd and, without saying a word, wrapped his arms around her waist and kissed her.

*

This, she thought, was heaven. A lifetime could have passed within the measure of the next days, the worries she'd brought with her seemed to be distant memories of another life. A life without John. Not long before their first night together, she'd realized he was a great guy, but never imagined what a man he really was: tender, smart, and sexy—very sexy.

"How did you get to be this way?" Audrey said, pulling up the sheets and resting her head on his chest. "I mean, in bed."

"I am afraid to ask, but I'm hoping the syntax of 'this way' means good." John played with a strand of her unruly hair.

"Amazing."

"You make me this way."

Maybe he was trying to be charming, but their chemistry was undeniable. Untamable. She'd never felt so comfortable with anyone and, because she'd never felt particularly skilled in the area of mind-blowing sex, she had to agree. It could be their utter connection or their love, maybe those were one and the same, but with him there was never awkwardness, and even the tip of his fingers gliding over her skin gave her immeasurable pleasure.

Along with their hunger for each other, their intimacy grew with each conversation. She'd never believed in soul mates, but if it was true there was one person in the whole world who was ideally suited to another, she'd found hers. Their connection ran deeper than the feeling she had when he touched her skin. She accepted, with no fright or anxiety, he was meant to own her heart forever; even if he no longer wished to.

They left Tuscaloosa, performed in Houston, and were on their way to Dallas. She was tired from the road and longed for a proper bed. Once there, they would be able to rest for three days before having to hop on the bus again and head out to Austin. When they stopped at a fast food restaurant on I-20, she carried her laptop in and thanked God for free wi-fi. After downloading the pictures of the past two gigs from her camera, she noticed a considerable increase in traffic on the band's Myspace page. She was surprised to read a comment on the page congratulating John for finding his muse, and it went on to say the song he wrote was beautiful, but the person who wrote the comment was in Oregon. Oregon? How in the hell he had heard the song if John had played only once? She scrolled down the comments and they'd mentioned the song again and again. YouTube? She searched it on YouTube and there it was: band's guitarist serenades his girlfriend in Tuscaloosa.

"Oh shit, you guys have to see this." Audrey and Kevin sat at a four top table, Matt, John, Tyler and Rob sat at the next one.

"Some YouTube user. . . ." She squinted at the laptop screen. "jewelsundquist11 recorded John's song and uploaded it the day after the gig in Tuscaloosa." She turned the laptop toward them. "Look at the view count."

It had 1,827,843 views. Tyler whistled in surprise.

"If those were sold records, we'd be platinum." Matt moved the laptop to his table and read some of the comments aloud. "I would serenade too if I had a girl like that; These guys are hot; this song is so beautiful, I can feel his love in every word; you made a mistake, dude, now she has the ball; what is the name of this song I want to buy it on iTunes."

Matt lifted his head and everyone looked at John.

"North Star," he said.

Matt continued to read. Most of the comments were favorable, and they wondered if some good would come out of it besides ad revenue for jewelsundquist11.

*

The news the band was going to record "North Star" in a professional studio in Austin took everyone by surprise. Bill had called and was meeting them there. Atlantis Records was interested in producing a single and a music video before deciding on a record deal. In a state of ecstasy, that night was their best performance to date. She heard "North Star" for the second time since Tuscaloosa. This time the band played it together, and Kevin sang it.

While she took the band's pictures, people in the audience took hers. It was surreal. Random people would come up and talk to her and ask how it felt having a song written for her and how was their relationship. Was viral fame so powerful? Clearly it was, and clearly she wasn't prepared for this kind of prying, but as much as she wanted to tell them to piss off, she knew she couldn't.

Suddenly worried, she hoped they could stay inside the bus forever, traveling the country, making out in twenty-four-hour Laundromats, and waking up in his arms in cheap hotels. She knew it was impossible. She knew they were good. She knew he was great and would quickly outgrow this life. The tour was about to be over; Austin was their last city. Would the band drive back home as planned? How would Bill react to meeting her? He would probably send her packing on the spot. She needed a drink; actually, many drinks.

By the time the band finished the encore, in which John had to play the acoustic version of "North Star" by popular demand, she was tipsy. When she saw the boys coming over, she quickly shook off the worries, gave them high fives and kissed John, causing a little stir among the watchful eyes nearby. She had already ordered them tequila shots and, as always, they toasted to the next gig.

"Is everything okay?" John must have sensed something.

"Sure," she lied.

Usually after a few beers and some chitchatting with the locals, Audrey and John escaped to enjoy some privacy, but that night it took them longer than usual to slip out.

"What are you thinking?" John said, breaking the silence. They barely made it to the hotel room, and after they'd wrinkled the sheets beyond ironing, they lay quietly for a long time.

"We will be in Austin tomorrow. It's such a beautiful city."

"Maybe we can go to the lake while we're there."

Audrey's voice dropped to a murmur. "Maybe."

Chapter 11

Austin. Live music capital of the world.

They drove straight to the recording studio downtown, where a pale-skinned, round-faced, and rosy-cheeked Bill was waiting. He had incredibly narrow eyes, as if distrust was one of his physical features. His thin auburn hair was tousled and looked like a crumbled sheet of cellophane paper. He gave prodigal hugs to the boys, and a special congratulatory hug to John.

"Audrey, I'm delighted to meet you."

"Thanks." She shook his clammy hand.

"I've got rooms at the Driskill for all of you, just a few blocks away." Bill nodded due west. "Audrey, why don't you go ahead and check in? The boys and I have to go over the details of tomorrow's recording session."

"Oh, no." Kevin grunted as a little boy whose mother had turned off his video game.

"She doesn't have to go." John cut through the semi-circle they formed in front of the building to stand beside her.

"She is our good luck charm," Tyler said.

She frowned at him, thinking it sounded too much like a pet.

"Of course, she can stay. I only thought she would like to rest." Disconcerted, Bill placed a hand on his hip.

"Bill is right. I'd like to rest." She was irritated by being talked about as if she wasn't there.

"Audrey can out-party any of us," Matt said.

Out-party? Was she a drunk now? She preferred to be the pet.

"Come on, Audrey, you don't want to be in the boring hotel, right?" Kevin said.

"Okay, let me think . . . hot shower and a mini-bar or jabbering with you . . . uh, see you later." She wanted to stay, but she had a gut feeling it was a bad idea to fall on Bill's bad grace so early in the game.

She turned to John, and the rest of the group seemed to take it as a sign of the end of the discussion.

John circled her waist with his arms, and whispered in her ear, "Please stay."

"Go to work and I'll be waiting for you at the hotel." She placed her arms on his shoulders. "I have some stuff to do." She kissed him.

"Don't start the drinking without us." Kevin shouted to Audrey who, already walking away, waved two fingers in the air without looking back.

She remembered the way John had spoken to Bill when he called early in the tour, presumably complaining about her meddling with the band's engagements. It was not surprising Bill would try to get rid of her as soon as he could. Actually, there was only one reason he didn't give her a check and bid her farewell: John. She thought of Bill's sticky hand and hers felt disgustingly tacky; she rubbed it hard on her jeans. It seemed his wide smile and educated talk about the business helped him nail his claws into as many upcoming bands as he could. She feared if the band's viral fame hadn't happened, they would have accomplished very little under his perfunctory management.

She crossed the street and her phone rang. Retrieving it from her backpack, she saw her mother's picture. Great mom, perfect timing, she thought, mildly annoyed.

"Hi, mom," she said, her voice as sweet as molasses.

"Hi, darling. How are you?"

"Super."

"What's wrong?"

"What do you mean?" She hated how her mom could read her so easily.

"You sound upset."

"How do you figure that? I said two words!"

"Must I remind you, I gave you life? I know everything about you."

"Mom, must I remind you that sounds very creepy?" Three minutes ago, she hadn't felt like talking to anyone, least of all her mother. Now her laughter made Audrey feel immediately better.

"So, how's everything?" Isabel tried to sound casual, but there was an inquisitive undertone to her voice.

Damn YouTube! From that point on, Audrey told her about everything she'd been doing since their last conversation, except anything related to John. She went on describing the towns to food to pubs to people.

"John! I want to know about John." Isabel interrupted with utter impatience.

"How do you know about him?"

"You're kidding? Everyone knows. Thanks to YouTube, I now know of cousins I never knew existed—in Brazil."

"No way!"

"Nice song, by the way."

*

Sometime later, Audrey noticed John leaning on the door of the bathroom looking at her inside a bathtub nearly overflowing with bubbles. She'd left him the second key at the front desk and didn't hear when he walked in.

"You look like a mermaid."

"Then maybe I can charm you into joining me."

He lifted himself from the door, sat on the edge of the bathtub, and took off his boots. Then, he unbuttoned his shirt and unbuckled his belt slowly without letting go of her gaze.

"If you want to torture me, you're doing a superb job."

He got into the tub and sat across from her. They stared at each other with conspiratorial eyes. She wanted to feel his weight on top of her while she scratched his back with her nails; but she sat still, holding his gaze, showing him she, too, could play this game.

After what seemed like a thousand lifetimes he slid toward her, but she stopped him with her right foot on his chest. He moved her foot to his side and, beneath the water, his hands reached for her calves, traveled slowly up her legs, and squeezed her thighs. She knew she couldn't escape, neither did she try to. He moved very close, held her hips, and positioned her on top of him. Her back arched from the anticipated clench and the room—the world—was painted with the sensuous glow of skin and heat.

*

They spooned in bed and dozed off to the murmurs of the TV. Her body was pliable and buoyant from the hot bath and hot sex. She lay beside him with her head on his chest and eyelids heavy. The light touch of his hand rhythmically tracing her spine; up and down, down and up, made her realize he didn't share her state of mind.

"What's on your mind?"

"Just thinking about tomorrow. Atlantis is sending Glen Ballard to make new song arrangements for 'North Star.'"

"Glen Ballard?"

"He is a top songwriter and producer from L.A. An executive is coming as well to talk about the contract. The studio wants to speed through the creation of the single to take advantage of the video's popularity."

"I checked it when I got here. The view count is at almost three million."

"The guys and I told Bill we want to use your photographs."

"You shouldn't have. You must use whatever is the best for the band," she said, unsentimentally. "But thanks." Her face softened into a doubtful smile.

"You're welcome." John kissed her forehead, and she placed her head back on his chest.

"They want me to sing it." His voice was suddenly murky.

"This is ridiculous. They are taking this too literally." She propped herself up on one elbow.

"I agree, but it seems the circumstances of the song are as popular as the song itself, if not more." John seemed calm, but his voice had an exasperated undertone.

"How did Kevin take it?

"Not very well. No one would. This single can put us on the map."

"I'm sorry." She sat beside him.

"Hey, you." He moved one leg around her and hugged her from behind, resting his chin on her shoulder. "The only thing you should be sorry for is taking too long to be in my life."

"Oh, yeah?" Audrey felt the warmth of his body and her own temperature rise as his crotch pressed against the small of her back.

"Sure. Let's see, the first time I saw you three years ago to the first time you kissed me a week and a half ago. I think you have a lot of catching up to do."

"You were dating back then. What was her name, the blonde pygmy?"

"She was five-four."

"And you're what? Six-two? She looked like your personal stool."

"No matter, I've always thought of you."

"Whatever, Casanova, I am not a home wrecker," she said with feigned indignation. He tickled her, she squealed and turned around, pressing her body against him. One thing led to another.

*

Forty-five minutes later, she was still thinking about the day they met. The band was playing in Michigan and she'd driven there to see Matt for the first time since they were children. She had felt immediately attracted to John. He was tall with wide shoulders that tapered to a narrow waist, and a sculptured face with strong cheekbones and contoured mouth. He wasn't a boyish male-model kind of beauty; his rugged looks screamed untaught confidence. They'd barely talked that night. She was there to catch up with an old friend and the rest of the band was very occupied with the swarm of girls that circled around them, including the blonde pigmy. Audrey had toasted with them: tequila and a lime wedge. Life was good.

"My heart stopped when I saw you, but Matt—"

"He is like my brother."

"I didn't know that. Besides, he didn't talk about you like a brother." They lay sideways on the bed facing each other.

"Because he is a guy, and that's what guys do. Did you know we kissed?" She bit her lips and watched John's eyes widen. "We were eleven. Playing spin-the-bottle. We didn't open our mouths but when his lips got really close to mine, he exhaled profusely. I think he was so surprised the moment we were told we had to kiss, he held this breath and forgot about it until he was right in my face. It was awkward between us until the end of the school year." Audrey stared at John with fascinated curiosity. "But, uh, I'm pretty sure we were each other's first kiss." She giggled.

He turned on his back. "Great."

"But. . . ." She stretched her hand and twirled a finger in a curl of hair below his navel. "I'm pretty sure you can be my last."

*

Later, the band, Rob, Audrey, and Bill had dinner together at the hotel's restaurant. It was exceptionally awkward for her. Bill watched her and John closely, as if he was playing a Jenga game, except he searched for the exact piece to remove so the tower would topple down on itself.

Kevin was trying to be his old I-don't-have-a-care-in-the-world self, but he was uncharacteristically quiet. Being removed from center stage was not the way he dreamed of recording their first hit. They didn't talk much about work and everyone went their separate ways right after dessert.

The night was clear and warm, so she and John decided to go for a stroll. They walked together, his arm on her shoulders and hers on his waist, and talked about how they'd come to know Austin. He had gone to Willie's Nelson Fourth of July picnic in 2000 and she had an aunt from her father's side who lived in Round Rock just north of the city.

"So I've been thinking," she said.

"Hm?"

"Since I'm already down here, I could spend a few days with my aunt." Audrey planned to stay with her if the band was diverted from its original route the day after tomorrow.

"But we're most likely leaving the day after tomorrow." He gave her a concerned glance.

"The band is leaving, sure, but the tour is over and so is my job...if you can call it that." She wanted to wait and see what was going to happen with the band, but she also didn't want to become an imposition.

"I beg to differ." They stopped at the corner of the street waiting for the light. He turned to face her. "We need you now more than ever. You can continue to be our photographer. I imagine we'll need tons of marketing material if we sign a record deal."

"The studio will have professionals do that."

"You're a professional."

Audrey snorted.

"The photographs you took are really good and that's what matters. Besides, what's professional anyway? You do your job very professionally; you're a professional." John looked into her eyes without a hint of irony.

She let out a soft sigh of defeat. It seemed impossible to say anything that would persuade him to let her go.

"Everything is going to work out." He placed his arm back on her shoulder and they crossed the street.

*

The next day, they met at the studio at nine o'clock in the morning. Glen was scheduled to arrive at ten-thirty and the band wanted to rehearse before he arrived. John would not leave the hotel without Audrey who, in spite of herself, joined him and taking her laptop, figured she could answer the band's emails and edit her photographs. The bagels, fruit and cheese platters, and plenty of coffee were a firm indication they had a long day ahead of them.

She showed Bill her photographs while the band rehearsed in the sound room. Before the slide show she'd prepared was over, he got up from his chair and poured himself a cup of coffee.

"I must thank you for 'North Star'." He sat on a big chair about five feet behind her.

"Well, you don't have to thank me for that. I didn't write it."

"But without you, it would never exist." He sipped his coffee. "And now, because of the wonders of Internet, you're attached to it forever." She guessed the grim tone in his voice was a firm indication of how he felt about her relationship with John.

"I don't follow you. It's just a song."

"No, my dear, it's not. It would be if three million people hadn't watched him singing it to you. If they hadn't seen his face and your tears. Walking off the stage and kiss? Classic!" He finished his coffee and tossed the cup in the trash like a basketball.

"And this is a problem why?"

"Because this song is only good as long as you two are together." He stood up and started to walk toward the door. She could hear men talking on the other side; it seemed Glen Ballard and the Atlantis Records' executive had arrived.

On his way to the door Bill stopped beside her and placed a hand on her shoulder. "And we all know how long relationships last nowadays, especially the ones involving rock stars and groupies."

Her blood boiled and outrage surged in her veins, but before she could open her mouth he was shaking Glen Ballard's hands and smiling like an orphan who had just been adopted.

The band came out from the sound room and introductions took place by the food table. Glen wore khakis and a navy V-neck sweater. He was incredibly tall and bulky, like an antique wooden wardrobe. He introduced himself to everyone with a deep voice that rumbled at each handshake. The executive's name was Tim Stein, and he spoke very softly in comparison to Glen, more of a joy-of-painting kind of guy than an executive from the brutal music industry. Bill followed him around throughout the day, a purring kitty cat.

"So, you're 'North Star'." Glen held Audrey's fingers lightly.

"Hardly." She ran her other hand through her hair.

He kissed her hand, walked toward John, and asked, "Do you know why this song—and video—is such a hit?"

John looked at Audrey, but before he could say anything, Glen continued, "Because it was sincere and heartfelt, just a boy telling a girl how he felt. I wish I had thought about that." A communal laugh swept the room. "But I didn't and I don't believe you did either until you were up there doing it." He looked at John. "Just a boy and a girl." His voice faded out like the end of a CD track. Then he clapped his hands together and said. "So, where do we start?"

Audrey returned to her seat and continued to read the comments on their website. Glen, Bill and Tim went inside the sound room with the band. Glen sat on a stool and listened to their ideas. With the door open, she could hear their conversation.

"Kevin is our lead singer. He should be the one recording this song. I can't reach the high notes he can." John announced after Tim explained Atlantis's idea for "North Star."

"I understand and I agree with you. From the demo Bill has sent me, I can tell you don't have Kevin's emotive falsetto." Glen proposed to record a version of the song in which John and Kevin would almost perform a duet, leaving the latter with the high notes and the chorus.

They worked for fours hours straight and only stopped to eat when a catering company changed the breakfast table to lunch. Audrey photographed them recording, and Tim asked to see her photographs from the tour. He told her they would be able to use some of them on their promotional material. He asked her what her employment status was with the band. So corporate, she thought. What he really wanted was a title. Kevin, who was in front of them in a line for the potato salad, overheard and said. "She is our muse and drinking buddy."

"How sweet, Kevin. I'm truly touched." She elbowed him on the back.

"She is our chief executive officer of public relations, strategic planning, and visual imaging." Matt was eating chips standing on the other side of the table.

"Congratulations, Matt, you've made up the longest bullshit title in history." Audrey said.

At that point, everyone in the room was listening to their conversation.

"I can tell you one thing, toasting after a finished gig has been much better when you have a hot chick waiting for you at the bar, and the girls think we're sensitive when they see us partying with another girl," Tyler said.

"Amen to that, brother," Glen said.

"Like you ever needed my help to hook up." Audrey glanced at Tyler and he gave her a vehement shrug of the shoulders. "And for your information, girls who hook up with musicians at bars are not looking for sensitivity."

They laughed.

"A liaison between the fans and the band is something many performers have these days to help them keep up with the fans in the social networking age. The fans are also crazy for behind-the-scenes photographs and videos." Tim said.

"Who better to do this job than someone who's already been doing it—very well—without pay." John stretched out the word 'pay'.

"Oh, we have to rectify that." Tim looked at Bill, who twisted his face up in a mournful smile.

Tim turned back to Audrey. "Bill had told me you were leaving after the tour."

As Audrey, John, and the rest of the band turned their gazes to Bill, he said, "Circumstances have changed, apparently."

"Are you available to go to L.A.?" Tim asked her.

"Absolutely." Her eyes met John's, and he gave her a radiant smile that seemed to say: I told you so.

Chapter 12

Los Angeles—the place where rock stars were born was, of course, the next logical step for the band. Atlantis was there, and the amount of money spent on the band suggested the good-faith agreement Tim had them sign soon would be followed by a contract. The band and Audrey were settled in a house for out-of-town artists in Silver Lake, from where they could see a miniature downtown L.A. It came complete with pool, hot tub, and a guest-house converted into a studio, fully equipped and soundproofed. After a day to get settled, the band was off to the Atlantis offices to perform for several executives.

With "North Star's" recording wrapped up, the band was off to shoot its music video. They were taken to a warehouse where a large area was covered in green screen and illuminated by flood lights. As it turned out, most of the scenes with the band would be shot in front of the green screen, and later on, graphic artists could create a computer-generated background.

Audrey was introduced to the director of photography, a tall and handsome Brit named Edward. The perfect black 007: strong cheekbones, broad shoulders, and charming accent.

"I'm not really a professional photographer," she explained while shaking his hand. "My education is in art history." Her tone was apologetic.

"Mine is geography." He was a very kind man and a generous professional who didn't hesitate to share tips of the trade. In exchange, she answered his questions about the band's members, which he assured her helped him to establish a connection between his subjects and the camera. She tried to take in everything Edward was willing to give; cameras he liked to work with most, his thought process, other photographers who might have influenced his work, and even gossip on some of his celebrity clients. They quickly hit it off, and he invited her to observe how he worked in his studio, where he promised there were a scandalous amount of equipment and props.

She'd never seen a professional photo shoot before; actually, she didn't even think there were cameras as big as the one Edward was using, but she discovered later a battery pack was attached to it. She had taken photography classes in college, those involved spending many hours inside a darkroom burning and dodging her photographs to bring the images of poorly shot negatives to life. She would not even have a digital camera if her father hadn't given her one a few Christmas ago. He had been generous—and a little pushy—to give her a Nikon SLR with high pixel resolution, telephoto lens, and a set of filters.

"You take beautiful pictures, sweetheart. You should do it more," He said after she unwrapped her gift. It appeared he knew she was unhappy long before she realized it herself. It wasn't that she hated her job; rather the problem was she didn't know what she loved to do to earn a living. Otherwise, she knew exactly what she loved: travel, art, cook, going to the movies, tequila. Unfortunately, the last time she checked the classifieds, there was no job for a tipsy arts critic who was available to travel and that could cook a mean chicken parmesan.

*

By midday, the shooting hadn't started yet and, after a while, it felt as if the taping of a four-minute video was like untangling dreadlocks: nearly impossible and very painful. She was particularly amused because, judging by the sheer amount of green screen, this video would probably be completely redone on a computer. She'd instantly become more appreciative of full-length movies.

John walked out from the dressing room, and said, "what are you doing?" He plopped himself beside her on the couch in the makeshift waiting area across from the green screen.

"Twittering about your big Hollywood day."

"Imagine what would take to make a full-length movie? No wonder they spend months at the time on locations."

She gave him an incredulous look. "I was just thinking that."

"Great minds think alike." He kissed her neck below the earlobe. "Do you think we can find a more suitable place to elaborate?" He mumbled between kisses, breathing so close to her skin it gave her goosebumps.

"I think due to the importance of the subject at hand, we shall try." She nibbled at his lips and got up. John followed her to a side door where she had seen some of the crew going in and out earlier.

"John." Just as they reached the door, the costume director, a stubby middle-aged woman, called out from the dressing room. "We need you to try your outfit with the rest of the band's. Got to make sure they're all good on camera."

"Be right there." John sounded as enthusiastic as a teenager going to the orthodontist. He kissed Audrey and whispered in her ear, "hold that thought."

On her way back to the couch, she stopped at a table covered with pastry, fruit, and a caterer-style thermos of coffee.

"Audrey, how are you?" Tim and a young woman approached when she was filling up a foam cup.

"Well. You?"

"Great. Has the shooting started yet?

"Not yet."

"I meant to be here earlier." He turned to the woman. "This is Jennifer, she is one of our P. R. associates and she will be working with the band." Jennifer was lithe and petite, like a Barbie doll.

"Nice to meet you." Jennifer touched Audrey's hand the same way one would pull strips of dead skin from a sunburned back.

"You, too."

"I love 'North Star'." Jennifer measured Audrey up from head to toe. "You're so lucky."

What the hell are you looking at, Audrey thought, but said,

"Yes, I know." She smiled, trying to dilute the tinge of irritation in her voice.

"Where are the boys?" Tim said.

"Trying on their outfits." Audrey nodded toward the dressing room.

Tim looked at Jennifer. "Let's go talk to them."

"See you later." Jennifer walked away, giving Audrey a conceited smile.

Welcome to Hollywood, Audrey thought, then sipped her coffee and resumed her place on the couch to fiddle with her phone.

It was almost four in the afternoon when the cameras started to roll. John and Kevin had to lip sing to the version of "North Star" they had recorded in Austin. Audrey could tell they were uncomfortable, but after a few takes, they performed more naturally. They played for hours, moving around to accommodate the new position of the cameras. For the close-ups of each band member, the others had to stop playing and move out of the way completely. The band had to walk from the back to the front of the green screen-covered room so often she had lost count. Later, a production assistant told her the video's concept was to have the band—especially John—walking in the desert at dusk following the stars. Because the green screen wasn't long enough, they would have to piece together the footage to the length it needed to be. They must have played "North Star" at least fifty times that afternoon, and when the director finally yelled "it's a wrap," it was almost midnight.

Two days later, Bill called to let them know the shooting had been a success. The director had all he needed and it would only take a few more days to put the video together. Atlantis was making the graphic artists work around the clock. Then Bill, saving the big news for last, told them the band was to perform live on the Ellen Degeneres Show.

*

She wondered what she would do all day; it couldn't be completely boring to watch the band on a live show and, hopefully, meet Ellen in person. Audrey had always liked her stand up comedy routines. Ellen had to be extra clever to come up with funny material while still keeping it clean from the racist, sexist, and dirty jokes many other comedians relied on. But she was tired of following the band, and never completely forgot what Bill had told her in Austin. He was a douchebag who had no idea of whom she really was—not a groupie, that's for damn sure. Nevertheless, the prospect of being called a "groupie" on national TV gave her the shivers.

"We have to leave in an hour," John told them after he hung up the phone.

"Good luck, guys." She looked up from her newspaper. They were all in the kitchen, Matt had made a pot of coffee that was quickly drained by everyone, Kevin ate cereal from the box sitting on the counter, and Tyler sat at the table reading the comics.

"Uh, Bill said everybody." John walked to the coffee maker and started to work on a fresh pot.

"I'm sure he meant everybody in the band."

"Maybe we should get you to play percussion, Audrey. What you think of a tambourine?" Kevin said, his mouth completely stuffed with cereal.

She grimaced at him and shook her head in disagreement for both—his comment and his lack of manners; then turned to John with pleading eyes.

"Sorry, babe, Bill said 'Audrey too.'"

"What would you do all day, anyway?" Kevin had pulled out the orange juice from the refrigerator, and lifted the carton to his mouth but, having realized everyone was watching, stopped himself.

"For starters, I wouldn't have to look at your face." She stood up and walked away; behind her, they erupted in guffaws.

*

When John walked into the room, she had finished showering and was sitting on the bed towel-drying her hair.

"Hmm, live TV show. What should I wear?" He turned from the closet holding two black T-shirts, differing from one another only by their degree of fading. She loved the way he dressed: solid-color Ts or V-necks under button-down shirts in some sort of subdued plaid with the sleeves rolled up above his elbows, never sporting prints or logos, and low-waist jeans; not so low the jeans clung to his ass by paranormal powers, but low enough she could sneak a peak of his midriff whenever he lifted his arms.

"If Bill asked for me—specifically—he's up to something." She was wearing a cotton bathrobe that came with the house. After a long moment of silence, she stopped working out the tangles in her hair to look at John. She followed his gaze to discover he was looking at the contour of her left breast, visible through the opening of the bathrobe.

"John?" She turned and sat cross-legged facing him.

"I don't know. Maybe he just wanted to make sure you didn't feel left out."

"How thoughtful." She tried, unsuccessfully, not to roll her eyes.

He walked around the bed and sat behind her, his expression was one of concentration. Perhaps he would be able to make sense of the situation. He slid one hand inside her bathrobe and ran his fingers lightly over her breast. She couldn't help but giggle.

"Get out of here." She pulled his hand away.

"I'm thinking!" He protested.

"You have been playing for nearly ten years, have written hundreds of songs, and you know the only thing they will talk about on that show is that damn YouTube video, don't you?"

He twirled a strand of Audrey's hair around his finger, looking at it pensively. "Everyone starts from somewhere."

"How did you come to be so wise?"

"Ha." John chuckled. "I guess all the partying and drinking I've been doing with the band for the past eight years have served me well."

"Something did." Was it possible some people were born with the kind of wisdom that others had to search for their entire lives?

"I'm not wise, babe. I just know sometimes sacrifices must be made."

John was off-the-charts smart, read Nietzsche and Kafka and knew all that there was to know about music, from blues to classical and everything in between. Would it be enough to protect him from fame? From money?

*

The band spent on stage one-tenth of their entire day at the Warner Bros studio. Everyone stayed in a green room for most of the time. A production assistant took the band to see the part of the studio where they would perform. It was separated from the main studio by a huge sliding wall, on the other side the audience was being perked up by another P.A. who explained to them how the show worked after the cameras were rolling. Later on, Ellen herself went to meet them. Slim and vibrant, her face looked older than on TV, but still much younger than her actual fifty-something-years. She was witty and sweet, asking them about home and if they hated L.A yet. She had heard their music and congratulated them for the success, assuring she was going to buy a CD as soon as it was released. Audrey was taken aback by how down to earth Ellen was and, for an instant, she hoped this wasn't going to be the circus performance she feared. Unfortunately, right before another production assistant whisked Ellen away, she also told them how cool was the YouTube video and she was going to use it to call Audrey on stage before the band played.

"What?" Audrey's eyes almost jumped out of her face. The P.A. rushed Ellen to makeup while she assured them someone would explain everything.

"Can you believe it?" Audrey gave John an incredulous look.

"At least she told us now." John didn't show a shred of enthusiasm.

"Did you really expect anything different? And the single hasn't even been released yet." Kevin said.

Audrey glanced around the room into each of their faces and they all looked like they'd been tossed into an icy lake.

"We might as well make the best of it now." Matt gave them his never-blue smile.

Tyler stood up, his chest puffed up like a medieval king about to talk his warriors into battle. "If they want to make us look like an amateur stunt gone right, let's show them what we're made off." Then he walked to the food table in the back of the room and grabbed a bunch of grapes.

"That's right." Matt said halfheartedly.

"Everyone starts from somewhere, uh?" Audrey mumbled to John.

Someone knocked on the door; the same assistant who took Ellen away was there to usher Audrey to makeup. She got up and let out an enormous sigh that made the boys laugh. The assistant looked confused and mildly annoyed.

"Cheer up, you don't want to be a big grouch on national television," Matt told her as she exited the room, giving the door a contained slam.

*

There was probably some way their TV appearance could had been worse. Like, for instance, if the band had no instruments, and they all had sat around Ellen and chatted about Audrey's sex life. Her entrance was right after Ellen played the YouTube video at the time John walked off the stage. Ellen announced to her audience this love demonstration had already surpassed three million views, "and here she is, the girl everyone wants to be…"

Hooray!

Ellen asked Audrey how they met, what it was like to be the only girl on a bus with five guys, etc. The upside of Audrey's appearance was when Ellen showed some of the photographs she had taken on tour and mentioned she was a photographer.

After the band finished playing "North Star", Ellen led Audrey from their chairs to the stage where the band was. She stood between John and Audrey, and asked John a couple of jovial questions: how hard he thought it was declaring himself to a girl in front of an audience, and if America should expect to follow their relationship with new songs in a hopefully soon-to-be released CD. John told her, in a very gracious manner, despite "North Star's" popularity, the band's eight-year-long career had given them a large enough repertoire to compile a CD without any more information about his relationship.

All Audrey could think was during the time Ellen had spent asking her irrelevant questions the band could have played at least another song. Although the boys seemed satisfied with the outcome of their first national television interview, in her heart Audrey knew this kind of attention meant trouble.

Chapter 13

Their TV appearance was quickly followed by the release of "North Star's" music video, and it propelled the band to instantaneous stardom. In light of their success, Atlantis signed the band and their first CD was to be released soon. Bill took them to a dealership to celebrate; as a perk, Atlantis had leased cars for everyone. The very sweet American dream—at least, the bit about material prosperity.

"Me, too?" Audrey asked as the salesman led them through the lot and asked her if she liked any of the cars she saw.

"It has been already arranged," Bill said sourly.

John gave her an endearing smile and the thought of him making requests to anyone on her behalf gave her a pang of chagrin; especially to Bill, who had made clear she was no more than a groupie. Kevin, Tyler, and Matt ran between the rows of sports cars, spotless and incredibly shiny as if a washing crew had just left the lot.

"John, I'm not sure about this." Audrey told him when he followed her toward the less glamorous line-up.

"You can't survive in L.A. without a car." He caught up to her and laced his fingers on hers.

"I don't feel comfortable. I haven't earned it."

"Earned it? Babe, seriously? Do you feel guilty for accepting a little perk from a multi-million dollar corporation that probably writes it all off in tax deductions?

"My mother always said it's better to make your own journey by foot than riding on someone else's horse." Audrey chuckled. "It's a Brazilian thing."

"Hmm, interesting."

"I grew up watching my mother's side of the family live in Brazil with so little money and yet they were the happiest people I knew. They didn't want to buy a newer car every year, or the largest flat screens available, or the biggest house on the block.

They were happy with their comfortably restrained life as long as they could spend it together."

"It sounds like a utopian society. How about education, careers, uh, the corporate ladder?"

"All of my three uncles went to college. One is an agronomist and has a farm near my grandfather's, the other two are business owners. My aunt has a PhD in mathematics, and she teaches at a Federal University. They're not at all the starved and uneducated aborigines portrayed on the six o'clock world news."

"Our media is not the most reliable source for world events, especially the ratings-driven news broadcasting shows." John pulled Audrey toward a Mercedes SLK and said, "Check this one out."

"Absolutely not." Audrey shook her head, looking at the fiery red convertible with tan leather interior.

"You would look very sexy driving this." He pinned her against the car kissing and nibbling at her neck.

"I love when you do that." She whispered.

"How about this?" He bit her earlobe.

"That too."

"And this?" He trailed the side of her neck with his lips and delved his tongue in her ear.

"Ahem." Bill cleared his throat from a few feet away. "The boys already made their choice: convertibles."

John looked expectantly at Audrey who said, "How about that one?" She pointed at a lonely Toyota Prius sitting on an unpopulated corner.

They drove to the beach and along the way she parked at a gas station and rode with John to have dinner in Malibu.

*

The fact that their newfound fans seemed to get much more of a thrill from John's love life than from the band's songs didn't seem to bother anyone but Audrey. Inevitably, she had to accompany them in all their appearances.

"KYSR wants to interview Audrey, too." Bill told them one morning. She and Matt had arrived from their run. John was reading the newspaper at the kitchen table, and Kevin and Tyler were still sleeping.

Surprised, she stopped with a bottle of water midway to her mouth. The room was quiet except for Tyler's soft snoring coming from the living room. He had been demoted to the couch since Bill had taken his bed for the days he was in L.A., claiming he had back problems.

"Why?" She looked at Bill.

"You know why." He spoke condescendingly.

Matt sat at the table and picked up the sections of paper John had discarded.

She looked at John and Matt who were both staring at her, took a big gulp of water, and said, "Look, Bill, I don't want to tell you how to do your job."

Bill was standing in between the kitchen and living room toying with his cell phone, when Audrey's words sank in, he shifted his weight, disconcerted as if she had cuffed him on the ear.

"But you have to stop this madness. Get the focus back to the band and leave me out of it."

Bill cleared his throat. "Audrey—darling—please know having you involved in the band's professional engagements is not my preferred marketing strategy."

Audrey suppressed a snort. Right, like you ever had a 'marketing strategy.'

"Great, then. Just tell KYSR and whoever else asks for me, no."

"That's impossible—unfortunately."

"Yes, it's very possible. I won't go." She shrugged.

"If you don't go, you'll give them reasons to inquire about the stability of your relationship, and, potentially, start attracting another kind of attention. Much more unpleasant, I must warn you." He walked to the coffee maker and poured himself a cup.

She hated to agree with Bill, but he was right. It was hard to stomach the situation, but it would be harder if she had to deal with gossip about a break-up. She'd have to suck it up. After all, she was living the life most woman would kill for: going to Hollywood parties, hanging out with musicians, and being loved by the man she loved.

"Don't worry, pretty soon it will all be in the past and the boys will be able to continue their career without, uh, 'North Star's nuisances." The corner of his lips slightly tweaked upward.

Did he say what she thought he did? Audrey wanted to knee him on the crotch.

John stood from his chair and walked toward her, circling his arm around her waist from behind. He kissed her neck, lifted his gaze to meet Bill's, and asked, "What do you mean?" His face pressed against her head and his arms curled around her like a protective shield.

"Uh, a second hit will give people something new to talk about it." Bill gave them his million-dollar smile.

*

Audrey had continued to work keeping up with their fan mail, but there was no need for a photographer with the band at all times. They spent all day everyday inside the studio working with producers to select songs from their repertoire and composing new ones. And these were just the demos; recording would officially commence only when they had chosen the twelve tracks or so for their album. She felt as useful as a calendar from a previous year.

Several of her photographs—heavily retouched on Photoshop— made into the publicity package for the band, but she suspected Atlantis was hiring a real photographer for the upcoming CD and eventual tour. Regardless of their decision, she wanted to move on. She needed to learn more to even consider offering her services as a photographer. As a matter of fact, she still wasn't sure it was what she wanted to do. Until Tuscaloosa, her life had been a boring story unfolding in front of her. She couldn't wait for everything to fall into place anymore. One thing was clear: she had found John and lightning doesn't strike the same place twice.

For self-preservation, she'd never spoken in advance about things she planned to do, she would rather wait until the deed was done. It eliminated unnecessary explanations and unfulfilled expectations. Like bringing a boyfriend home only if they remained together after the novelty of the initial six months had faded. However, she intended to spend the rest of her life with John, so this was a good chance to exercise sharing her plans with someone before she acted on them.

"I'm going to visit Edward today." She told John from the shower while he brushed his teeth.

"Mm-hmm." He was swishing mouthwash.

She cracked the shower curtain open and said, "I want to ask him if I can come over more often…to learn…like an apprenticeship."

John turned toward her, his mouth parted slightly by surprise.

She closed the curtain and said over the shower, "I don't want to sit at Atlantis all day answering fan mail anymore." She waited for his response, fighting the urge to look.

A few moments later, John opened the shower curtain and stepped in. She smiled as he took the soap from her hand.

"We'll be performing more very soon, and we'll need you," he said, soaping her shoulder, then her back as she turned. "I can talk to Tim. You can do something else."

"John, I don't want you to find me a job."

"I know."

Taking the soap and switching places with him she said, "I need to find my own way."

"I know," he mumbled, grabbing the bottle of shampoo. "I—I'm just gonna miss you."

"I know." She took the shampoo from his hand.

He rinsed his hair in silence, then kissed her.

*

At the studio, Audrey watched Edward and his assistants working on a photo shoot for an upscale clothing catalog. She talked to Janice, his secretary, for a while, and after he called a lunch break she approached him gingerly, almost ashamed to ask.

"Apprentice?" He snorted it and she wished she hadn't opened her mouth. "I haven't heard that in so long. I feel very Da Vinci all of the sudden."

Audrey made a mental note not to say that word near him ever again.

"How about an assistant, Audrey? Part-time. Low pay. Heavy lifting. How does that sound?"

She swallowed hard and her eyes burned from the imminent tears she hoped to hold back. It was the best news she'd gotten since John had said he loved her.

"Perfect." She hugged Edward.

"You'll pretty much be carrying equipment around, so don't hug me just yet."

She didn't care. She was going to be a photographer.

*

After the band signed the contract, their status as out-of-town artists was revoked and they had to vacate the house. As much as Audrey loved the guys, she longed to have a place just for her and John, where they could walk naked, cook together, and settle into coupledom and domesticity. However, she said nothing. Surprisingly, the suggestion to live separately came from Kevin, who said he wanted to have his own place to escape the artistic influence from the others—especially John—and find himself again. The biggest load of bullshit he had thrown at them yet; but, conflicted herself about what life in L.A. would do to them, she had to give him the benefit of the doubt.

Though Matt and Tyler disapproved of the new living arrangements, they were Audrey and John's biggest supporters. It would also be nice for them to have a place of their own, where no woman would be telling them to pick up after themselves as she did sometimes. The four of them looked at apartments together. Audrey suspected Matt and Tyler had hoped to find two available apartments in the same building complex, and so did she. After looking in North Hollywood, Silver Lake, and Brentwood, she and John settled for a small bungalow in Pasadena; then Matt and Tyler rented a loft a few miles away.

The Spanish-style bungalow reminded her of the farm house in Brazil, with stained alabaster stucco exterior, red terra-cotta tile roof and a matching color front door. Sunny orange California poppies framed the sides of the stone steps leading to the graceful arched-opening porch. The sun-drenched backyard was landscaped with purple sage, lavender, and more California poppies.

During the next weeks she and John made the bungalow their own, like a corny television couple who had just moved to their first house. They painted together and ate pizza sitting on the floor in an empty living room.

"Are you sure about this?" John asked her as he rolled deep burgundy streaks of a color called Vin Rouge on the wall of their master bedroom.

"It will look good against the white crown moldings and some black and white photography." She pointed at the walls and described to John where the art would go.

They bought a few practical pieces of furniture at IKEA: a dinette table with chairs, bar stools for the kitchen counter, a geometric-print futon, pots and pans and a few other essentials. For the rest of the house, they would look for pieces that spoke to them.

On Saturday mornings, they looked for garage sales and visited antiquaries. The first piece of art they bought for their house, was a sixteen-by-twelve inch vintage illustration of a coffee cup with the words "coffee" and "bottomless cup" at the top and bottom of the image, and a five-cent sign at the bottom right corner. It cost three dollars, but she felt shamelessly happy. It was different from purchasing a futon, pots or pans; they'd bought something with no practical purpose whatsoever, a real indication of their commitment in building their home—their life together.

*

Kevin had been the biggest rupture to the living organism they had created since she joined the band on tour. He was quickly swept away by the shining lights of Hollywood. He was the first to rent his own place. He knew everybody, went to all the parties, and slept with all the models. Matt and Tyler were able to get a free ride on his wild train for a while, but they couldn't keep up. Even Tyler, the notorious womanizer, didn't keep a scoreboard like Kevin's.

A few months later, their CD was released and another track did well on the charts. While Atlantis put together a national tour, they'd started to perform locally, with gigs almost weekly. The spotlight shone back on Kevin, whose wild voice, dirty blonde locks, and charismatic personality always caused an enthusiastic uproar on stage. As Bill predicted, a second hit had cast a shadow on "North Stars's" incidental focus on their love life and John resumed his role as the guitarist. He seemed relieved to be detached from center stage as there were less and less requests for him to sing "North Star."

If for the world Kevin was the band's heart, in reality, John was its liver: filtering the junk into useful stuff for the band and, most importantly, creating the songs which made it all possible.

"I love your raspy voice. It's sexy." She refilled his glass of wine and watched his face change colors, his shyness never ceased to amuse her.

"I could never do it." He sipped his wine and flipped over the chicken breasts on the grill. "I like to sing, but what Kevin does is much more than that, it's a performance. Like acting."

"You did great, though."

"For one song yes, but imagine an entire concert. I'm sure the audience would get tired of me closing my eyes or staring at nowhere. Kevin engages the audience and more they give him more he gives back."

"True. He thrives on attention."

Chapter 14

The job was not as bad as Edward had told her. Sure, there was plenty of heavy lifting, but she could do much more. Photography at Edward's level had nothing to do with what she'd seen in college, and working in his studio was like being on the set of The Devil Wears Prada: she'd never seen so many wonderful and unwearable clothes. The models seemed like creatures from another planet; incredibly tall—even next to her five-eight—emaciated to the point of tears, and very pale. They would arrive at the studio wearing no make-up, with their hair pulled in high ponytails, holding bottles of water, and talking on their cell phones.

In the mornings, Edward would huddle with the assistants and talk about the assignment they were about to work on. Then they would set up the lights and backdrop according to his specifications, along with the cameras, lenses, filters, and computers. By the time the shooting was about to start, the studio looked like Grand Central Station at rush hour with makeup artists, stylists, magazine editors, models, caterers systematically moving through a chaotic pattern.

Edward taught her about lighting, temperature, white balance and many other singularities of digital photography, such as RAW files. She listened to him as if her life depended on it, and in a way it did. It was the first time she had a chance to learn from a real photographer, and it was Edward McCalman nonetheless. He was coveted by the largest magazines in print, anything from fashion, music, and travel. Other than Annie Leibovitz, one of her favorite contemporary photographers, he was the most popular photographer in fashion, at least on the West Coast. He often worked on locations, and surprisingly the cinematographic work he did with the band's music video was not the bulk of his business.

"I have this dinosaur here if you want to play." He led her into a storage room in the back of the studio and opened a bag with a Zenza Bronica inside.

"Oh my goodness—the same medium-format camera they had at school. They are great."

"Indeed. I quite enjoyed it, but it's unrealistic for commercial work now. I don't even have a darkroom anymore. You can rent one; I know an excellent place down Sunset."

"Thanks."

"Sure, no problem. I have to go check my schedule with Janine, but feel free to browse here. I'm sure I still have unused film somewhere and I think its tripod is over there." He pointed to a cluttered corner of the room and left.

Her voice dropped paradoxically low to the intensity of her awe. "All right."

For once, she wasn't swimming against the current. Immediately, she thought of her mother and wondered if this was what she meant by "let God govern your life," because she felt none of what was happening in her life could possibly be by her own doing.

She rummaged through the room and was able to put together a kit for the Bronica: lens, light meter, film, filters, and tripod. She thought about what Edward had said, and the key word was—commercial. Her education was in Art History, she wasn't sure she was cut for commercial photography. The frantic rhythm of Edward's studio put her in a whirl, and she didn't want feel like that for the rest of her life. Working with film gave her a sense of control and she hoped to eventually find her way.

*

"Hi, mate." Charlie, an expatriate from Ireland and Edward's main assistant, greeted her when arriving at the studio after-hours. Because of Edward's assignments in different parts of the country and abroad to which he took one of his real assistants, she was able to use his studio to take her own photographs, in an attempt to unveil the secret of photography—light.

"Hi. Are you going to use the studio too?" Audrey said, kind of embarrassed. Charlie was an excellent photographer, very hip and with a subtle Irving Penn sensibility for gritty, high-contrast photographs.

"Nope. I've just finished a session with Jeremy Renner for Men's Health."

"How was it?"

"Great. He's very grounded, none of the 'I'm-a-movie-star' bullshit."

"Did you go alone?" She ended up assisting him more than she assisted Edward, who was like one of the great painters of the Renaissance whose apprentices labored over the majority of the work and the master validated it by swiping its final brushstroke.

"Yeh, it was at his house, very laid back. He invited me to the L.A. premiere of his new movie."

"You're on fire, Charlie. I know pretty soon I'm going to see you in front of the cameras instead of behind them." He was known to enjoy sharing many pints with a new wave of young actors, and his thick accent, flamed hair, and wild temper preceded him. He was even credited with a few famous portraits of rising movie stars whom he'd befriended in L.A.'s night scene.

"Acting?" He snorted. "No way, but I wouldn't mind directing a motion picture some day. Anyways, I'm on my way to a drawing session at the Getty Center, just stopped by to get my stuff. Wanna come?"

"Drawing?"

"Yeh, I have a friend who works there and a group of employees gather in a studio to draw from a live model after work."

"Sure, sounds cool." She knew John was coming home late because the band was rehearsing for their upcoming tour.

*

The Getty Center was an impressive construction. It must be what Mount Olympus would look like: a white castle surrounded by gardens and clouds on the top of a mountain.

"How long have you been coming here?" Audrey asked him while riding the tram up the mountain to the museum. The five minute ride was beautiful as long as she concentrated on one side of the view; the other side displayed traffic on Interstate 405, which epitomized one of L.A.'s biggest nightmares.

"I dunno. Four months maybe."

She flipped the pages of his sketchbook. "You're really good."

"Thanks. I wanted to be a painter."

"Really?" Audrey looked at him in surprise. He was such a good photographer she would never had guessed it wasn't what he wanted to do all along.

"Sure. I began working with photography to make ends meet. Since I couldn't find a respectful gallery to represent me."

"You seem to be doing really well."

"No shite. Go figure."

"But you like what you do, right?"

"Yeah, love it. I don't think I'd ever give up photography now, even if my paintings would save the world from being obliterated by a blazing asteroid. The exchange yeh have when photographing people and the rhythm of a fashion photo shoot pumps me up," Charlie mused, his accent rising in intensity as he grew more excited. No wonder he was so popular, she thought. He was so lively, it must be hilarious to hang out with him at a bar.

"That's great. You know, doing what you love and excelling at it."

"I reckon if yeh do what yeh love, chances are yeh'll be good at it."

"And when you are good, people start to knead you up for money like a chunk of clay until you don't even know what you looked like before."

"Is that what is happening with the band?" Charlie asked.

*

The studio where the drawing session took place was underground and there were a gathering of interesting people who drew while listening to blues and drinking wine. Every fifteen minutes when the model had a break to stretch, she would put her robe on and walk around looking at the drawings. She was a petite and fair-skinned brunette named Megan who reminded Audrey of Carey Mulligan in *An Education.*

Audrey covered her sketch book and warned Megan, "I haven't drawn from life in a long, long time."

"Oh, don't worry. I'm used to the strangest depictions of me; it's what I like most about modeling." Megan smiled and Audrey uncovered her sketchbook. "It's good. It reminds me of an Egon Schiele."

"Yeah?" Audrey looked back at the drawing. "That is not a weenie, by the way. It's just a messed-up line; I don't have an eraser."

When the drawing session was over, she learned Megan had been in Brazil during a summer in high-school with a mission group from her hometown church, and had recently moved to L.A. from Tampa to get her MBA at USC. She told Megan about her new photographic endeavors and Megan offered to pose for her, should she ever need it. Audrey never thought of having models, it seemed so far-off from what she was seeing at Edward's studio—even though they worked with models all day, but in Edward's case, the work was so purposeful. Even before he turned on his camera, he'd already had the whole session mapped out: outfits lined out, makeup applied, light tested.

There must be a way she could put Megan's talents to good use, Audrey thought. Photo-essay? Pin-up style portraits? Whatever it was, she would have been crazy to dismiss her offer.

*

Audrey's first photographs with the medium-format camera were black and white long exposures in downtown L.A. The images created the atmospheric ambiance of a town populated by ghosts— blurred shadows of people across an unidentifiable cityscape. She had done similar work while in school using a Holga, the twenty-bucks-worth plastic camera gave her extraordinary results and, by accident, she learned the effects of photographing at night. Now with Edward's fancy Bronica, she could use filters to achieve the same effect at daytime.

"That's interesting." Edward was looking at her first batch of prints.

"Really?" she asked shyly.

"Absolutely, I like this one with the rain, it's really moody. But what I like most is it doesn't even look like L.A, and I can't tell where it could be."

"I tried to remove all landmarks. I wanted to create a quintessential urban landscape where these forms floated aimlessly."

"Uh." Edward looked intently into the pictures, rubbing his temple with one hand.

"I-I mean…this is kind of how I feel here."

He put the photographs down and pulled out his cell. Audrey didn't know what else to say; she was starting to feel self-conscious. Edward dialed a number.

"Hey Ben. It's Edward…How's it going, mate?…I'm doing great, quite busy actually…Oh, yeah?… I'm going to Nice for Louis Vuitton next month…I know, I'm looking forward to it. Hey, I'm sending you an artist I want you to meet."

Audrey's eyes widened.

"She has some 16x20 silver print I think you should take a look at…She's new in town… No, not represented yet."

Edward looked at Audrey who shook her head.

"When are you available?...Hold on, let me check."

Edward moved the phone a few inches away from his mouth. "Are you free tomorrow around lunch?"

"Yes."

"Lovely, she'll meet you there," he said, speaking into the phone again.

He glanced at her, sitting at the other side of the desk.

"Yes, very...Okay, bye." He hung up, smiling.

"Ben has a gallery in North Hollywood. He can be a flippant arse sometimes, but he is mostly harmless." He picked up the pictures again. "I bet you fifty bucks he'll ask you out," he said in a cautionary tone.

"I'd hate to waste his time," Audrey said, half to herself.

"But you have some good work here. I think you should show it to him, perhaps he can do something. He'll see you tomorrow at one."

Audrey didn't say anything, her eyes fixed somewhere beyond the walls, her expression blank.

"Audrey, I know sometimes we feel we're not ready and the work we put out is not good enough. Believe me, every artist has had the same exact thought. At some point, you just have to put yourself out there and see what happens."

"I suppose you're right." She looked at him and smiled.

He showed her one of her own photographs and said, "You have a definite voice and something to say in here. Don't take that lightly."

"I appreciate it, Edward." Audrey was truly thankful for his words. She wanted to hang on to them like a mother holds a newborn baby, tenderly, carefully, so nothing will ever come to harm it.

*

In nearly five months in L.A, she witnessed how much the very dynamics of the city seem to work to keep people away from each other. It could take two hours to drive ten miles because of the mind-blowing traffic. But when she left Ben's gallery in North Hollywood, not even that could ruin her mood.

I AM TAKING YOU TO DINNER TONIGHT, MY TREAT. She texted John as soon as she got in the car. It turned out Edward was right, Ben had asked her to dinner to "discuss further" the terms of his gallery's representation. Luckily, he had already bought two of her photographs for five hundred dollars each, and invited her to participate in a group show at the end of August. Audrey politely told him she had plans—with her boyfriend, and saw his enthusiasm burn out like the flame of a jar candle covered by a heavy book.

Not long after she started the four-wheeled dance toward the interstate, her phone rang.

"I have good news," she said.

"Tell me." John said.

"You're talking to a represented artist, who's sold two photographs."

"I knew you had this one, babe."

"Thanks. And I'll be in a group show in October."

"Cool. What about?"

"Time." Audrey was so happy the thick mass of cars as she merged onto I-134 East didn't phase her. "Do you want to go to the Argentinian Place on Green?"

"Oh, babe. Bill is getting into town tonight and we're all supposed to have this dinner with Tim and Jennifer to talk about the new tour."

"Oh."

"Jennifer told me only thirty minutes ago. I was about to call you. I didn't want to interrupt your meeting. Why don't you come with us?"

"Business dinner? With Bill?"

"I'll tell you what. I've heard we're eating at the Polo Lounge. Supposedly, Tim loves the chef there. I'll get us a room and we can celebrate afterwards."

"At the Beverly Hills Hotel? John, it's too expensive." Even as she said it, she felt a surge of excitement tingling her fingers.

"I think the occasion calls for it."

"Hah, you're the one on the top charts. We didn't do anything special when you got signed."

"Yes, I think we did."

She blushed and remembered them walking out of a storage closet inconspicuously after a quickie at a bar in Silver Lake. The band and Audrey had made friends with the bartender while living at the Atlantis house. They'd gone there to celebrate and the bartender had let them use a back door to go outside and smoke in peace, since the front entrance was always jammed with people. She didn't smoke, but she had walked out with John, and his eyes changed when she took a drag from his cigarette, still in his fingers.

"You're so sexy," he said as she exhaled the smoke. She'd helped his hand between the buttons of her dress, threw his cigarette out, and led him to the—doorless—closet she'd noticed on their way out. From a dark corner of the room, behind a shelf stocked with cleaning supplies, they could hear the waiters walking on the corridor. If any of them had made a left turn instead of right, in search of paper towels or a mop, he or she would had been in for a big surprise. John was motionless, completely taken aback by her initiative. She felt powerful, invincible. When she unbuckled his belt, he pleadingly murmured her name, but she muffled the sound taking his mouth into hers, then knelt down and his entire body quivered.

She put the phone on speaker as a police car passed her. "That was momentary insanity, it doesn't count."

"'Momentary insanity?' Isn't it what guilty people say to get out of trouble?"

"Innocent until proven otherwise."

"Come on, babe. We deserve it. But if it makes you feel better, I might be able to write it off as an expense."

"Getting corporate savvy already?"

"I'm trying to make lemonade," he mused.

"Okay, sure. It will be great. I just hate to see you spending money unnecessarily."

"I'd give all I have."

Chapter 15

On the Fourth of July weekend, Matt and Tyler rented a house in Malibu and threw a party on Saturday night. The house was starting to fill up. Bill had flown in with his wife, and Kevin brought his latest hook-up, a model he'd met in a magazine's after-party. They stood in the doorway between the living and dining room, Kevin's face woozy, his fingers playing with a string on his date's peasant blouse.

Matt and Jennifer were sitting on the couch, giggling. Jennifer? Huh. She didn't look like the kind of girl who would go for the sweet-and-nerdy type. Sharp and sleek, she seemed like the type of woman who would favor power-suits and thick wallets. Audrey tried to dismiss her judgmental thoughts and hoped Jennifer would be sharp enough to realize she had the best seat in the house. Then she continued to look for John, squeezing past a group of unrecognizable people into the kitchen. She saw Tyler leaning against the kitchen table, talking to a couple of girls he must have fished out from the beach, both wearing shorty shorts and bikini tops.

"Have you seen John?" Audrey asked, opening the refrigerator.

"Uh-uh." Tyler answered without taking his eyes from the girls.

Geez, thanks for the attention. You know how to make a girl feel special.

She grabbed a beer and sauntered back into the living room. A gust of ocean wind coated her face as a couple walked in through the sliding doors that led to the beach. Looking in that direction, she saw John and Bill smoking on the deck, ashtray on the rail between them.

"Audrey!" A voice cut across the room, stopping her mid-step. Her heart sank. Sharon.

Bill's wife hustled over, all lips and cleavage, and Audrey groaned inwardly as Sharon's acrylic nails touched her arm.

"Isn't this wonderful?" Sharon waved her half-empty margarita glass at the room.

"Yeah." She could be referring to the party or the house, but Audrey chose the answer she hoped would stop Sharon from elaborating. Since they'd arrived at the beach house, Audrey had listened, exhausted and bored, to Sharon's life story: marriage, Bill, divorce, marriage—to Bill, liposuction, boobs.

Audrey glanced longingly outside, John and Bill still had their backs to the house. She wished she could communicate to John telepathically and ask for help.

"You need a refill." She looked down at Sharon's glass.

"Girl, you're one of mine." Sharon winked and squeezed Audrey's arm.

Hardly.

Audrey smiled and pulled her arm away as Sharon wobbled to the kitchen looking for the pitcher of margaritas.

Audrey rushed to the door as if swimming away from a shark. When she stepped outside and the breeze danced around her, she closed her eyes and inhaled deeply. Finally, John was only five steps away.

"I'm just saying, this is not the best time to be in a serious relationship. You can have any—" Bill was talking while fanning himself with the collar of his shirt when he saw her.

Audrey stopped between the second and third step, caught somewhere between hurt and anger.

"Babe." John snagged Audrey in an embrace.

"Am I interrupting?" She didn't take her eyes off of Bill who stubbed his cigarette and looked at her, expressionless.

"No, of course not. Want to go for a walk?" John said.

Audrey nodded, and as they walked down the wood steps toward the beach, she heard Sharon squeaking at Bill.

*

The sky was the color of amethyst, the last rays of sunset lingered in the horizon. They walked on the beach with their arms locked around each other, her hand in his pocket and his on her waist.

"What is going on?" she asked soberly.

"Nothing. Bill is just being Bill."

"You mean, a sleaze-bag prick?"

"Yes, pretty much." He chuckled.

Audrey could tell he was tired, exhausted really. John had always been the one taking care of everyone, mediating the conflicts and dealing with the problems. Maybe he'd had enough, and for an instant, she felt her throat close up by the thought she could also be part of the reason John seemed unhappy.

"John, uh . . . if something is bothering you, if you're not sure . . . just tell me. I know a lot has changed. I—I want to see you happy."

He stopped, hugged her and kissed her forehead, his tender, shy eyes sparkled underneath his long eyelashes.

"The only thing I'm sure right now is that, for the rest of my life, I don't want to be apart from you—not for a second."

"But Bill—"

"Bill?" John snorted. "A guy like Bill can't begin to comprehend my feelings for you. Why bother explaining?" He moved his hands gently across her spine. "The only thing I needed him to understand is I'm not going to be Atlantis's puppet."

She rested her head on his chest and she could hear his heart beat. She closed her eyes to take it all in; the warmth of his breath on her hair, the strength of his arms around her, the smell of the ocean in front of them. She didn't believe in prayers like her mother did, but in that moment, she sent out a thought to the Universe hoping someone, something, will hear it—and answer it.

Please keep this man, this good man—my love—from suffering.

*

Despite Bill's presence hovering over John like a vulture circling around a carcass, the party was not bad. After the sunset, fireworks exploded sporadically in the sky, coloring the sand and waves red, white, and blue. Neither Megan nor Charlie showed up, so she talked to some of the people she knew from Atlantis. She also recognized some of the girls, models she'd seen at Edwards, probably friends of Kevin's date.

"Matt, I haven't talked to you all night." Audrey met him at the fridge when they both went for another beer.

"I don't want to talk to you. You're taken." He handed her a beer, twisted his own open, and threw his arm around her shoulders.

"I see how it is, unless I serve your specific purpose I'm not good even for frivolous conversation." She shook his arm off of her as they strolled off the kitchen.

"I'd be glad to chat—but—I've spent half of the night chatting with a girl who is as unlikely to sleep with me as you." He gulped his beer. "I have some catching up to do if I want to get laid tonight." He clicked his beer bottle on hers.

"Are you talking about Jennifer? I thought you guys had hit it off."

"Nope." He leaned closer and whispered, "I think her bells ring for someone else," then, turned his head, and Audrey followed his gaze to the corner of the other room. Jennifer was talking to John and a couple she didn't recognize.

Her blue eyes flickered at John and her body language was all about seduction. She tossed her hair to the side and slid her fingers down her neck to play with a pendant sitting above her breasts. Then, her hand touched John's arm and she laughed as if he'd said the funniest joke in the world.

"You're kidding, right?" Audrey said.

"Right." Matt grinned sarcastically and made his way to the porch where Tyler was sitting with Bill and a bunch of other people.

Chapter 16

It was great to have a woman friend, especially someone who wasn't involved in the music business. Megan was hilarious, with a blunt sense of humor accompanied by a surprisingly dirty mouth. Audrey loved it.

"I love this song," Megan said when "North Star" started playing on the radio while they were driving to go get a drink after a drawing session. Charlie was on an assignment, so the night was testosterone-free.

Audrey smiled, but didn't say anything. She had told Megan she had a boyfriend, but not who he was. So far, L.A. had been about the band and "North Star's" consequential focus on her love life. Audrey was just getting away from the media's scrutiny. She didn't presume she was a celebrity, but she damn sure was not going to attract any attention to who her boyfriend was, and that his success was propelled by a song he wrote for her.

"How come you didn't come to the party?" Audrey said, thinking if Megan had made it her comment about "North Star" would be different.

"My parents came to visit me. They feel guilty because they've booked a cruise for Thanksgiving."

"So, they came celebrate Thanksgiving in July?"

"Pretty much." Megan snorted. "I got totally screwed. Had to hang with mom and dad on the sexiest holiday of the year and I'll have no family during the most boring holiday of the year."

"How about Valentine's Day? Isn't that the sexiest holiday of the year?"

"No way. Too much pressure and freaking winter. Fourth of July is all about drinking, having sex on the warm sand, and watching fireworks while you come."

Audrey pictured the image and had to agree with Megan; it was appealing. Unfortunately, due to Bill's jackass remark to John, she hadn't felt sexy at all when they walked on the beach, but they had their night of passion after she'd whisked him away from Jennifer as soon as she saw her hanging around him like a cat in heat. She gave silent thanks to Matt for pointing it out, sometimes one needed help seeing the obvious.

At the bar, Megan seemed extra annoyed by the men constantly subjecting them to lame pick-up lines, and after they dismissed the third pair who'd come to their table, the conversation steered to sexual rights and equality.

"Men are incorrigible jerks. All they care about is pussy and tits," Megan said. "My last boyfriend cheated on me every chance he had. How about you?"

"I've never cheated on you."

"Shut up," Megan laughed. "You know what I'm talking about, so spit it out."

"My last boyfriend. . ." Audrey trailed off. It seemed like forever ago, she didn't really want to talk about it, but looking at Megan's eager expression, she had no choice. "Thought we were getting married."

"Oh, please tell me you ditched him at the altar. It's so Runaway Bride."

"No, of course not. I just let the relationship—and his nuptial plans—go on for quite a long time. I wasn't in love with him, maybe never was."

"How did you know?"

"Well"—Audrey ducked her head and took a long pull of beer—"I have a formula: tequila and Goo Goo Dolls."

"That's it? Get drunk and dump them?"

"Sort off. It helps me think, the alcohol takes the edge off reality while the music gives me the emotional groundwork to sort things out."

"How did he take it?"

"Not well. He accused me of taking advantage of his love and throwing him in the dumps without compassion. He called me a traitor in every form of the word."

"What a baby." Megan waved down the waiter and ordered two Mexican boilermakers.

"We stayed at it for two months, our divorce battle."

"You mean two months of hot make-up sex?"

"Hotter than it had ever been, but not worth it. I felt guilty. Spent of trying to explain I never meant to hurt him. One day he just got up and left. Never came back..."—Audrey sighed—"his heart broken beyond mending."

"Good for you, girl. I hate how men think we're all running against our biological clocks, ready to settle for anybody and procreate. You know what I think?" Megan picked up one of the shot glasses of tequila the waiter had brought over and looked at Audrey, who did the same. "Women should just walk around naked all the time." They knocked back the tequila, flinching at the burn.

Audrey squinted at her. "Huh?"

"It would simplify the entire process, because, at the end of day, men—all of them."—she waved her hand in a circular motion—"are only interested in how we look naked."

Before Audrey felt her brain swaying in tequila like a fishing boat on the open sea, she thought a series of portraits where Megan would be in various unsuspecting places—post office, gas station, grocery store—wearing only sexy underwear, would be a perfect opportunity to take up Megan's offer to pose for her. The idea seemed feasible if they acted quickly to capture everyone's reaction, candidly—Cartier-Bresson style.

*

She had stopped drinking when Megan called her roommates to pick her up. She offered to take Megan home, but was glad when Megan turned her down because waiting for her roommates had given Audrey a chance to drink a Coke and sober up a bit.

She'd texted John during the night. he'd been home for a while with Matt and Tyler. When she opened the door, they were in the living room.

"Hey, babe." John stood up and met her halfway. She'd felt tired on her way home, but the very sight of him activated her senses and made her temperature rise.

"Hey, you." She placed her arms on his shoulders and kissed him. A long kiss. His mouth was cool and tangy from beer. Her fingers stroked and pulled his hair lightly. She kissed his chin, grazed her lips on his five-o'clock shadow, and purred in his ear, "I've missed you."

"Oh, get a room." Tyler got up from the carpet.

"We better get going. Someone is a little drunk." Matt sing-songed as he walked past them toward the door. Resting her head on John's chest, she acknowledged Matt and Tyler with a brief smile.

The door banged behind them not a second too soon. Audrey kissed John so fiercely it was unclear when her mouth left off and his began. His hands traveled down, cupping her bottom and pressing her against him, igniting a fire that made her gasp. His tongue delved inside her ear and trailed down her neck.

Between pieces of clothing flying in the air and ardent fondling, John pinned her against the wall and reached for the door, turning the key in the lock. His hand slid between her legs and she tightened the hold on his shoulders, barely able to stand. Then, he lifted her up against him. She straddled her legs to accommodate him, clenching them around his hips and, crowded against the wall, moaned when he thrust inside her. Like a blind person whose fingertips brush over the patterns of a book in Braille, she could read his passion building up with her hands on the hard muscles of his back. He groaned only once, lingering inside of her for a moment longer when they'd arrived at the evanescent place of molten bones. If not for his arms around her, she would have oozed onto the floor. After his muscles relaxed, he hugged her tight and took her to bed.

*

No longer inside the tour bus, John seemed to have made peace that the situation they lived in, at the time they'd fallen in love, could not be prolonged indefinitely. They settled into a somewhat normal routine: leaving for work every morning, meeting for lunch sometimes, and coming back to their house in the evenings. The band performed mostly around the West Coast, but since she'd started to work with Edward, she didn't accompany them to every gig. It had only been a few months the "North Star" tornado had dissipated and she enjoyed the calmness.

She hadn't made any friends in L.A besides Charlie and Megan—the fault of her growing bias toward, basically, anyone who lived in the city. They were the only ones she'd managed to exchange numbers with and talk regularly.

Hanging out with Megan consisted of lots and lots of locker-room talk, almost as they were guys instead of, as she would say, gals.

"Oh, man I am so horny!" Megan said one day, so pensively Audrey wondered if that was what she really meant to say.

"Uh?"

"It has been months since I've exchanged any bodily fluids."

"Seriously?"

"Don't tell me, when you ravish your boyfriend, what's-his-name…?"

"John."

"Right, Johnny, you don't exchange—"

"Let's leave my bodily fluids alone, shall we?"

"Don't be embarrassed, it's what normal and healthy people do." Megan spoke in a solemn tone of voice.

"You know, I have some single friends, I'm sure they'll be more than happy to exchange, uh…with you."

"They? How many are we talking about?"

"Well, there are three. Unfortunately, I would rule one out, since I don't really see him that much anymore."

"Are they cute?"

"Super cute, but I take no responsibility for anything that happens after the introductions. And please, please, spare me the details."

"Fair enough."

*

Audrey knew she couldn't keep John and Megan in separate orbits of her life any longer. It had become difficult to keep John's anonymity since she and Megan became closer, and John had more than once asked to be introduced. So, she invited Charlie, Megan, and a curator from The Getty, along with Matt, Tyler, and Kevin to dinner at their bungalow.

"It smells good. What is it called again?" John asked, walking into the porch with napkins and silverware.

"Barbecue?"

"Isn't the Brazilian, what is it called . . . chubaka?"

"Chubaka? Churrasco, John. Churrasco."

Audrey's mother never liked the American barbecue her dad made—hot dogs and hamburgers. For that reason, Isabel was the one who'd commanded the grill in their household, imparting Audrey with a taste for the Brazilian flavor. But she was not going full fledge on the Brazilian cuisine that night, she was only grilling individual-sized skewers of meat and veggies—a better alternative from John's suggestion: hamburgers, which she found quite endearing since it reminded her of her parents, but very tailgate-ish for a dinner party. The idea of grilling was to make the dinner less formal, yet she refused to serve anyone hamburgers.

Matt and Tyler arrived with beer, but Audrey was drinking wine, the same Chianti she and John had on their first date, the night they'd said "I love you" only a few months ago. She'd never stopped to think how fast their relationship was going. It felt right, that's all it mattered.

"So have you guys christened this place properly yet?" Tyler smirked.

"Absolutely." She tapped John's bottom as she made her way to the porch with a tray of vegetables.

"I hope you did it in every room, or it's bad luck," Tyler said.

"Numbskull," John said, shaking his head.

Megan arrived, and Charlie, then Rachel. Megan didn't seem surprised when introduced to John, Matt and Tyler. Audrey had feared this moment would change their friendship, but now she was just relieved Megan hadn't recognized them.

After dinner, when Audrey walked into the kitchen to make coffee. Megan followed her, offering to help.

"Your friends are cute," Megan said, leaning against the counter.

"Yeah? I'm glad you think so." Audrey retrieved the coffee beans from the cabinet.

"John is super nice and very in love."

Audrey chuckled and said, "How do you figure?"

"For one, he wrote you that song."

Audrey faced Megan. "Oh, you've recognized them."

"No, I've recognized you."

"How?"

"I like Ellen DeGeneres."

"So, you've known all along? Why didn't you say something?"

"Why should I? You didn't seem eager to talk about it."

Audrey sighed. "Yeah, since we got to L.A. things have been so crazy, I don't really—"

"Audrey, it's fine. I can only imagine how awful it must be to have your relationship in the public eye. You're the new Brangelina."

"Except we don't have a mansion in France to hide out."

"Not yet." Megan snorted.

Just then, Kevin walked in, stumbling toward them.

"Hello, darling." He hugged Audrey.

"Oh, my gosh Kevin. You stink." She pushed him away.

"Uh-oh, mommy is mad." Kevin turned to Megan. "And who is this?"

"Hi, I'm Megan," she said, stretching her arm out.

"Kevin." He kissed her hand. "But you can call me Kev," he said, holding Megan's hand to his lips.

"Kev?" Audrey flinched. "I'll get you some coffee." She couldn't remember the last time she'd seen him sober.

"Coffee? Ugh." He made a face of disgust and walked away.

"And that is Kevin." Audrey watched him wobble off to the porch. "At least the L.A. version of him."

"L.A. can be a life-changing city."

"No kidding."

Chapter 17

A distant ring steered Audrey back to reality as John reached for the phone on the nightstand. She'd been dozing off, nestled beside him in bed, and nothing in the world felt better than his naked body against hers.

"Hello?" He sat up suddenly and turned on the lamp. Startled, Audrey pulled up the blankets to cover herself.

"Are you hurt? Where are you?…I'll be there as soon as I can." As he hung up, he turned to her. "Kevin has been in an accident."

"Is he okay?"

"He is fine, but he was driving under the influence and was taken to the police station in West Hollywood."

"I'll come with you."

On their way out of the house, Audrey called Matt and Tyler and they arrived at the police station almost simultaneously. While they waited for Kevin's release, John talked to a police officer who said Kevin refused to take the sobriety test but was clearly intoxicated.

"If you're really his friend, I recommend you have a real good talk to him." The officer shook John's hand. "He's a young kid, shouldn't be playing with his life like that." He spoke paternally.

Audrey watched the officer disappear behind the door and thought he should be in his late fifties—about her father's age. More than likely with kids and a wife who prayed every night for her husband to return home unharmed.

Kevin was brought in, scuffed and wrinkled. He looked rough and beautiful. Audrey gave him a hug while Matt and Tyler tapped him on the back.

"What the fuck were you thinking?" John was the only one who seemed unmoved.

"John, we'll talk about it somewhere else. Let's get out of here." Audrey touched his arm.

"I want to go to my apartment." Kevin muttered as they walked to the door.

"We're all going home." Audrey replied before John, looking furious, could say anything.

*

The heat coming in when Audrey opened the door for Jennifer the next day was stifling. She didn't know if it was just July in California or Jennifer's vibe.

"Oh, hi." Audrey was surprised to see her.

"Hi, Audrey. I came to talk to Kevin."

"Come in, he's still asleep."

"How did you know he was here?"

"I've called John."

John had run to the grocery store to buy coffee. After they got home from the police station, they drank plenty of it while trying to talk some sense into Kevin's head. Matt and Tyler left only when the sun came up. Kevin had passed out on the couch before that, but she and John never made it to bed.

She led Jennifer to the kitchen and sat across from her at the table. "I'd offer some coffee, but we ran out."

"It's okay. I don't drink coffee."

Really? It was hard to imagine life without coffee.

"I love your place," Jennifer said, sweeping the room with her eyes.

"Thanks." She looked into Jennifer's eyes and said, "I am so lucky," with a distinctive innuendo in her voice. Jennifer's expression changed and Audrey felt a deep satisfaction in knowing that, finally, they understood each other. For months, Jennifer behaved as if she mirrored Bill's feelings about Audrey: a groupie that had her days counted until John got tired and moved on.

"We used another one of your photographs," Jennifer said, and Audrey realized she was a tough player and subtlety was her game. "For a poster composite for the band's concert in Utah. You should expect a check soon."

"Excellent." She wasn't concerned about royalties at that moment, but she suspected Jennifer was waiting for John to arrive to talk about the repercussions of Kevin's accident. Thankfully, he was coming in through the kitchen door. Audrey remained seated with her back to the door and watched Jennifer preening in her chair.

Unbelievable!

"Hi, John."

"Hey, Jennifer."

"I'll start the coffee." Audrey stood up and surveyed the brown paper bags he had just lined up on the counter.

John unpacked the coffee and leaned toward her. "I can do it," he said, kissing her.

"Jennifer has been waiting for you. I'll do it. Leave the groceries, too; I'll take care of it." She reached for the coffee in his hand.

He pulled it away, circled his other arm around her waist, and kissed her again. "You're the best," he said, relinquishing the package.

Jennifer seemed anxious to start business, for John had barely let go of Audrey when she said, "Tabloids have got hold of Kevin's mug shot. We have to write a statement and also start thinking about community work. It's good for the band's image."

"We'll do whatever is necessary," John said, leaning with both hands on the chair Audrey had vacated.

"I'm sorry all of you will have to work."

"I don't mind, and I'm sure Matt and Tyler won't either."

"You're a great friend."

"Thanks." John shrugged off the compliment, while Audrey, unpacking the groceries, couldn't help but roll her eyes.

"Would you like some tea, Jennifer? We have green and chamomile," Audrey said, looking inside the cabinet.

"Oh, no thanks. It's too hot, but I'll have some water."

John straightened up and opened the fridge. "Here you go." He handed Jennifer a bottle of water and leaned against the counter, where Audrey placed two coffee mugs.

"I also bring some good news." Jennifer took a sip of water and patted her mouth with her fingers. "'North Star' was nominated for best video."

"The VMA?" John turned toward Jennifer who must have interpreted the gesture as the imminence of celebratory hug, because she stood from her chair and took a step closer.

"Yep, the list came out this morning." Her eyes fluttered with excitement.

"John, that's fantastic," Audrey said, and he automatically swiveled toward her, pulling her into a hug and lifting her off her feet.

"What's going on?" Kevin placed his hand on the door sill and swayed into the kitchen.

*

Thank heavens John was up early, because the phone wouldn't stop ringing. After the last call, she stayed in bed another twenty minutes, then gave up trying to sleep altogether. John made homestyle Eggo waffles for breakfast—his specialty. He'd toasted them medium dark, warmed the syrup, and cut strawberries for her. She loved playing house with him, now that the kids were out.

"So, what's all the commotion?" Audrey helped herself to the waffles while he poured them coffee.

"What commotion?" He said innocently.

"Did you get a direct fan line to our house? Because it seems like the kind of thing Bill would do just to piss me off."

"I guess everyone at Atlantis is worried about the band putting a good show at the VMAs tonight, including making sure we color-coordinate our ties."

Oh, shit. Audrey had completely forgotten about the award show. "Well I better get going then if I want to be back in time."

"Back? Where are you going?"

"To work. Edward is having me set up a Vanity Fair photo shoot in Santa Barbara. I've told you—"

"Santa Barbara? You're kidding, right?" A mix of frustration and disappointment seemed to scratch his voice. She walked to the bedroom and he followed. "I really wish you'd be there with me."

"And I will be, John, when I finish work."

"Work? Can't you take a day off?"

She looked at him in disbelief. Could it be that John didn't think her work was as important as his? But he looked as innocent as a child asking his mom for more dessert.

"Women take all day to get ready for this. It's almost ten o'clock and you have to go to Santa Barbara and back."

"What women, John? Singers, actresses, models? Well, I'm not any of that, am I? I am the fucking groupie who hit the jackpot." She looked at him, his eyes widened and his shoulders stiffened. Then she zipped her boots up and pulled her jeans over it.

It was like a volcano had erupted, now there was no containing the spread of lava. But John? He was everything to her. Before she could stop, she heard herself saying, "Oh, wait—I know, I am the hot Latina who must fuck him backwards so well, tons of gringos are parachuting in Brazil right now."

"Wait . . . a . . . minute," John stammered.

She felt the graze of his lifted, reaching hand as she stormed out.

*

The drive to Santa Barbara was the worst of her life, uncontrollable tears and sobs made the road barely visible. She pulled over to compose herself before showing up at the photo shoot looking so desolated. She replayed their fight over and over in her head. Not much of a fight really, more like a lion tamer opening the cage just to have his jugular ripped out of his throat by the beast he tried to domesticate.

She hadn't meant for all her anger to boil over onto the one person she had absolutely nothing against; on the contrary, she had learned to love him more than she knew possible. She didn't know what had taken over her, but living for months in a city where people used each other for their own ends and sucked their life for the sake of money had transformed her into something else entirely. Taken aback by her own cynicism, she wanted to turn around and go to him, but responsibility kept her headed toward Santa Barbara. She would go up there, set up the photo-shoot, explain to Edward she couldn't stay, and rush home. She thought of Jennifer's "you're so lucky" comments, which sounded more like "you're so unworthy," and felt a pang of regret because at that moment she really was unworthy of him. Loving John was easy, the challenge had been to feel she deserved to be loved back; not because he was an ascending rock-star—Jennifer's probable reason—but because he was inexplicably the one that made her feel whole.

Her mother's voice urging her not to sacrifice a career for a man was quickly dismissed by fear of losing him. She managed to get back to the apartment before five thirty, but he'd already left. Her heart turned to a block of ice, dropping onto the floor and shattering in millions of pieces. Be practical, she told herself. Get ready, grab a cab and at least try to get there as soon as possible. No answer on his cell; he must have been inside the auditorium. When she walked into the bedroom, already stripping to go shower, there was a box on their bed and a card with John's handwriting: in case you make it. She felt a pang of guilt thinking of him having to worry about the event and her awful words on top of it.

The box was white embossed with gold opposite facing C's overlapping each other. Chanel. A dress so beautiful it appeared to have descended straight from heaven. Pale nude in color, low cut cleavage, mid-thigh length, and completely embellished with delicate pearlescent sequins that seemed to be made from flower petals. When she put it on, for an instant, she understood the women John was referring to, who spent all day getting prepped—tanning, massages, facials, manicures and pedicures, hair, makeup—to slip into one of these.

She pulled her cell from the golden clutch that came with the strappy high heels also laid on the bed and dialed Jennifer's number from the cab.

"Jennifer, it's Audrey."

"Aw...hi, Audrey,"

"You sound disappointed."

"Oh no, just surprised. John said you weren't coming."

"He did?"

"Well—might—might not come."

"Is he around?"

"No, he is inside the auditorium right now. They close the doors to avoid people walking in and out on live TV. No cells allowed."

"I am on my way. How do I get in?."

When Audrey arrived at the Nokia theater she was surprised by the amount of people surrounding the place: fans, journalists, paparazzi, security, police. Audrey instructed the cab driver to stop near the back where Jennifer said she would be waiting with VIP passes at hand. The red carpet was empty, only a few publicists and crew recognizable by their black outfits, radios, blue-tooth headsets, and manila folders in their hands. Audrey walked toward the door hoping to see Jennifer among them, but she was nowhere to be found.

"That bitch!" Audrey mumbled. She called her again but this time there was no answer. She walked toward the door where a tall, shaved-head, almond-skin Samoan in a tailored black suit guarded the door with a grim expression.

Great, he turns away washed-up and wannabes trying to get in all day. What chance do I have, she thought.

"Hey, what's up?" She feigned nonchalance.

He glanced down at her, but didn't move a muscle.

"I'm looking for a P.R. from Atlantis Records who is supposed to meet me here with passes. Is there any way you could call someone to locate her? I'm terribly late and my boyfriend's band was nominated. I really don't want to miss it. Please."

"I'm sorry, ma'am. There is nothing I can do."

"Listen, I'm really not trying to crash this party. I hate this stuff, but the love of my life is in there—for the first time ever—and I've promised him I would be by his side."

The Samoan king let out a big sigh that filled Audrey with hope.

"Look, I can't let you in without a pass. Last time a beautiful woman wearing Chanel talked me into letting her in, she turned out to be a high-class hooker that offered her services to the last righteous celebrity in Hollywood and got me in trouble."

"How do you know I'm wearing Chanel?"

"Oh, girl. Pleeease." He intoned, pursing his lips. It turned out the Samoan king was a Samoan queen.

"I'm not a hooker, I promise." This was the one sentence she'd never imagined would come out of her mouth. Damn Hollywood.

"The best I can do is radio security inside and see if someone can locate this P.R. of yours."

Audrey slumped her shoulders and thought, shit! this will take forever. "Thank you."

After he did what he promised, he resumed his taut stance and grim look, and Audrey turned around and waited. She tried Jennifer's and John's cell again; nothing.

What can I do? She looked at her cell and had a crazy idea, all the while thinking: what are the odds?

"Charlie, it's Audrey. Where are you?"

She had just won the lottery. Charlie was there and he came to get her at the door, greeting Samoan queen with an enthusiastic fist bump.

"How come you're holding my mate at the gates, Ricky?"

"She didn't say she was your woman, brother."

"I'm not his woman." Audrey interjected.

Charlie and Ricky looked at Audrey, then at each other and started laughing.

Whatever. Audrey rolled her eyes. "Charlie, I really need to get in there before it's over."

"Go on in, girl. It's cool." Ricky waved her in.

She gave him a kiss on the cheeks. "Thank you. You're awesome and super-hot," she said already walking away. Ricky puffed out his chest so big; a little more and he might have exploded.

"You have a new best friend now." Charlie said, shaking his head. "Why are you stuck out here? I thought your song was up for an award."

"Well, I had to go to Santa Barbara set up Vanity Fair for Edward. Where were you?

"Edward knows I don't miss the VMAs. It's the craziest award in Hollywood. Musicians are party animals."

"How come your cell worked? I've been trying John's for hours."

"I don't go in the theater. Hate that shit. Americans have awards for everything. My ma always said doing a good job is its own award." He tossed her a tiny wink, and said, "I hang at the bar."

"Sweet."

They walked through a foyer, where a bar was set up football-stadium style, except there were tuxes and gowns in line for beer instead of jerseys and sports caps. There were high top tables spread around the area and people drank and talked while photographers and journalists browsed around looking for the most famous—those who congregated in private VIP lounges. Audrey spotted John, Matt, Kevin, and Tyler by a table. Jennifer was there standing beside John, not wearing the black suit that seemed to be the dress code for the publicists—men and women alike. She was wearing a skin-tight red gown with unbelievably low-cut cleavage and it looked amazing on her, the skanky bitch. No security would think she was a P.R. dressed like that, Audrey felt tempted to call Ricky and show him what a real high-class hooker looked like.

She marched toward them, breathing deeply like a defendant in court about to hear her fate from the judge, each step the sound of a drum beat in her ears. She was nervous; furious at Jennifer; but most of all, embarrassed. When she was about ten feet away, John spotted her. His eyes met hers and immediately lit up. She wanted to smile but shame stopped her. She looked at his face trying to decode his emotions: no anger or hurt. At that moment, looking into his eyes as they grew closer, she knew his restrained kindness, his immeasurable character, and his gentle touch smoothed every little crease of her soul.

"You look beautiful," John said.

"I'm sorry. I'm such an ass—"

He stopped her with a kiss and said softly, "we didn't win."

"That sucks." She stood on her tip-toes and hugged him tight. Over his shoulder she narrowed her eyes at Jennifer who matched Audrey's disdain, look by look.

Then, Audrey cupped John's face with her hands and kissed him hard, making all the boys jigger with excitement.

"Fuckin' hell. How long has it been since these two last saw one another?" Charlie said. The boys laughed and when Audrey finished kissing John, he was breathless.

"Thanks for meeting me at the door, Jennifer. If it wasn't for Charlie here I'd be outside—still."

John turned to face Jennifer, "Did you know she was coming?"

"Yes, it was a surprise." She smiled, then looked at Audrey and said, "I've been waiting for your call."

"I've called—several times."

"Did you?" Jennifer pulled her cell out of her wristlet bag over the table. "Oh, it's off. The battery is messed up, it keeps running out."

"Jennifer I've got to say, I'm disappointed. I expected more efficiency from you. Do not let it happen again." John said coldly.

"Of course not. I'm sorry, Audrey." Jennifer's face matched the color of her dress.

Chapter 18

The infamous party took place on a uncharacteristically murky night for Los Angeles in the house of Ryan Correll. One of Hollywood's rich-turned-celebrity by their superb job of making complete asses of themselves in front of a fair share of paparazzi. Ryan's headlines could pay the salaries of TMZ's employees, but he was not your average never-had-to-work-a-day-in-his-life millionaire. He was also the son of a media mogul who had been one of the founders of the movie industry—not the classy black-and-white movies, but the two-hundred-plus-million opening weekend kind. He was also a violent and self-righteous prick known for losing his temper easily. He'd had many dealings with the law and, currently, was stripped of his right to drive by the third DUI his father wasn't able to make go away. Thus, the parties now happened in his house on the Hollywood Hills, a place that made the Playboy Mansion look like an elementary school playground.

"Do we have to go?" She wound her fingers into John's hair and tightened the grip of her legs around his waist.

"Not really, but Matt and Tyler are expecting us." He bit her knee hard enough to make her let out a soft squeal and turned himself around to be atop her. She arched her back and let her thoughts race out of her mind.

They arrived at the party after midnight, and soon spotted Matt and Tyler talking to a group of people near a spectacular infinity pool. Not long after joining them, Matt and Tyler excused themselves to go get drinks and never came back. It took only a few minutes of listening to the three men and the woman in the group to realize why. Considering the looks of the other guests, she wondered why these—accountants— were even invited; hints were that Ryan had to invite some people from the studio to justify the party to his father as a business event.

Nearly half an hour passed, Audrey had color-coordinated the other guests, rearranged the furniture, and followed the trajectory of a fake lotus flower floating in the pool—twice.

"I haven't seen Kevin all night and I really need to catch him before he leaves." She stood up.

John gave her a pleading look, but before he could ask her not to leave him she was already walking away. She felt evil, but if John came, those people might follow and she couldn't stand them a minute longer.

She walked through the house. A considerable number of people was still at the party, but in the huge house they seemed sparse, mostly everyone scattered in small groups propping themselves against walls with red eyes, droopy eyelids, and low murmurs.

She toured the main level of the house, but there was no sign of Kevin. So she followed the long curving stairs to the second floor, trailing her fingers over the minimalistic paintings on the stairway. The house was decorated with sleek furniture and modern art; no family pictures to be seen. The accountants had mentioned when Ryan's parents moved to Santa Monica, they took their antique furniture and expensive works of art with them. She guessed Ryan must have posed a danger to their precious belongings, and everything was replaced with simple lines and bold colors. Yet, by the looks of it, they'd spent an obscene amount of money Ryan-proofing the place.

The first door at the top of the stairs led to a large master suite with a king size bed and a sitting area with a full couch, chaise lounge, chair, and TV. Three people sat on the couch, Ryan on the chaise, and two others on the floor.

Ryan turned his head toward her and slurred after a moment of silence, "Hey, come in gorgeous."

She walked toward them slowly, moving toward the center of the sitting area to have a good view of everyone.

"I was looking for—" She stopped when she saw a head of dirty blond locks hovering two inches from a coffee table. "Kevin?"

He lifted his head, but not before he inhaled the white powder laid on the table. "Hey, sexy."

She didn't think he recognized her at first; he must have taken her for one of the girls with whom he shared this new-found interest, but as his head bobbled back and forth with his glazed eyes fixed at her, he seemed to remember.

"Audrey . . . I was. . . ." He couldn't articulate.

Her legs weakened as color drained off her face. She didn't think a broken heart could be so heavy, but hers had fallen on the floor like a ball of lead. Her eyes skimmed the rest of the stoned faces and settled on Ryan's, staring at her with a grim expression. On impulse, she stepped toward the table, where a small silver tray still held half a dozen lines of cocaine, and slapped her hand down on the edge of it, watching as the people around her flung their hands up to ward off the spinning tray.

"What the fuck did you do, bitch?" Ryan jumped off his seat.

The cloud of white powder coated the furniture like dust.

"Fuck off," she said, leaning down toward Kevin.

Ryan grabbed her arm, and with his other hand slapped her face. Audrey shrieked and fell into the people sitting on the couch with a split lower lip.

"Come on, man." Kevin got up and pushed Ryan back with a hand on his chest, but Ryan pushed his hand down and threw a punch that made Kevin fly backwards over the chair onto the floor.

"You bastard!" She got up and punched his face, but it didn't phase him. Ryan grabbed her wrists and threw her back on the couch, vacated by the people who were already leaving the room.

"You cunt. You wasted two grand of good stuff," Ryan said, sitting on her and holding her arms.

She tried to fight him off, but he was too strong. He must have weighed over two hundred pounds, and she could barely move.

His grip on her wrists was so violent it burned when she struggled, as if she'd been handcuffed with fire.

"You'll have to pay me back somehow." His eyes were fixed on her panting chest, and he adjusted himself so that his cock pressed against her hips.

"Fuck you," Audrey snarled.

Kevin had curled himself in a fetal position, absorbed into a narcotic stupor, while Ryan rubbed himself against her so hard the buckle of his belt chafed her skin through her dress. She kicked and struggled, but he didn't budge. He leaned in and licked her neck.

"Get off me." Tears of anger and disgust formed in her eyes.

The next instant, Ryan flew off her and landed on the floor clear across the room.

"Are you okay?" John asked, helping her sit up. Before she could answer, he'd walked toward Ryan, who was just getting to his feet, and punched him. Ryan tripped over the corner of the bed and fell again, John kicked him on the stomach, grabbed his head, and slammed it on the floor.

"John, stop. You'll kill him."

He looked at the bloodied carpet, Ryan was already unconscious. Several people had been drawn by the commotion, including Matt and Tyler.

Audrey got up and went to Kevin.

"Call the police," John ordered Matt.

"No," said Audrey.

John looked at her, confused.

"It is not going to do us any good. Look at Kevin, he'll get in trouble."

They looked at Kevin's fluttering eyes.

"Let's get out of here," said Tyler, helping Kevin up. Matt grabbed Kevin's other arm and they walked him out.

John hugged Audrey, and his eyes welled up as he gently touched her swollen lip. "I'm so sorry," he whispered.

She placed her hand on top of his and said, very quietly, "take me away from here."

*

The shower hit Audrey harder than usual, her body ached and the cut on her lip stung as water ran over it. The skin on her wrists and her belly were grazed red. Her hips were sore. It really sucked to be a woman; a punch to Ryan's face with all her might didn't do more than tickle him. I should learn krav maga. Audrey smiled at the thought, then wept bitterly.

She palmed the condensation off the mirror, staring at herself, and let the towel wrapped around her fall on the floor. Above the sink, the reflection of her naked body stood still like a bronze torso on white marble. For the first time, she saw it as an object. Not someone, but something that could be groped by any asshole as long as his strength surpassed hers. It could be violated. Broken. She lifted her hands and cupped her breasts. Then, she heard the door of the bedroom open and quickly grabbed the towel from her feet and wrapped herself again.

John must have seen something awful in her face, because after gingerly entering the room, he was by her side in a split second. She pushed him away with her fists clenched on his chest, but he didn't let go. He held her tight and sobs overtook her. They sat on the floor, their backs against the sink, still for a long while.

"You should try to get some sleep." He said softly into her hair after she calmed down.

"No, I want to see Kevin."

"He's out. Passed out on the couch."

Audrey knew sleeping was impossible; adrenaline still ran in her veins like a lizard on hot asphalt. She put on a nightgown and a robe and they moved to the living room. She looked at Kevin sprawled on the couch and felt sad for her friend.

The sun was rising and the first morning light started to sweep into the apartment. Audrey poured herself a cup of coffee and sat with Matt and Tyler at the table.

"Are you okay?" Matt asked gently.

To comfort everyone, she mustered a faint smile. "Yes, of course. I am worried about Kevin. I never would have imagined he was so out of control."

"A lot makes sense now," Tyler said, without lifting his eyes from his mug.

When Kevin finally sat up on the couch, after waking up as slowly as someone regaining consciousness after a coma, he looked at his friends surrounding him. John was leaning against the fireplace's mantel, Matt and Audrey sat on the chairs across from the couch and Tyler stood between the living room and dining room. He glanced at them but didn't say a word.

"What is going on, man?" Tyler finally broke the stomach-churning silence in the room.

"What are you talking about?" Kevin said, leaning back in the couch, apparently, hoping nonchalance would help him.

"Please, Kevin. I think we deserve more than this," Audrey said.

They lapsed into silence again; no one knew how to start this conversation. They were in shock, as if they had just released a jammed seatbelt in a car accident and crawled out seconds before it exploded.

"You make it sound like you guys never partied before." Kevin crossed his hands cockily behind his head.

Audrey shook her head, disappointed.

John walked toward him with angry steps, grabbed him by the arm, pulled him off the couch toward her chair, and said, "Look at her, you son of a bitch. Does it look like she had fun at the party?"

Kevin looked at Audrey's swollen lip. Her bruised wrists rested on her lap, she tried to conceal the marks of Ryan's grip by pulling her sleeves down. He blinked hard and he said, "I'm so sorry."

She offered him her hand, he took it and nestled his head

against her lap. For once, she saw in Kevin's face traces of the genuine feelings often hidden underneath jokes and the sarcasm.

"I never meant to hurt you," he said, softly. "Any of you."

They moved to the kitchen and Kevin told them how he'd gotten involved with drugs. John had toasted waffles for everyone, Matt and Tyler were eating at the kitchen counter, and Kevin was drinking his second glass of orange juice.

"I was going out with Jess," Kevin said.

They all looked at each other confused—no one remembered who the hell Jess was.

"One of the models from the Elle spread, geez." Kevin rolled his eyes. "Remember, we all met afterwards at O'Maley's for drinks?" He looked at Matt and Tyler, waiting for confirmation. They shrugged.

"Has it been this long? That deal was over four months ago," John said.

"It didn't start that night, but the next time we went out it was just me and her. A date, you know? We went back to her apartment and that's when she offered me some." Kevin lifted his eyes, everyone in the room seemed half-dazed trying to make sense of this. Matt nodded absently, starting to look like a bobble head doll.

"We were making out on the bed and things were heating up, so she stops and pulls the drugs from her night stand, lays it out, rolls a dollar bill, and snorts it. And then she handed it to me—so casually. When she saw my hesitation, she said it would make it for the best fuck I've ever had."

"What an idiot," Tyler said.

"I liked her!" Kevin looked at John and Audrey as if searching for sympathy.

"Anyways, when I still hesitated, she said I was being judgmental. So I did it. And I continued doing it for the, uh, couple of weeks we went out. She introduced me to Ryan, and I started to get it from him. You can guess the rest."

"Do you owe him?" John asked.

"No—I dunno, maybe . . . two grand." He looked down.

"You don't fucking owe that prick a thing," Audrey said, standing from her chair and pointing her finger at him.

Kevin had assured them he wasn't an addict, and promised he could stop whenever he wanted, starting then.

"Atlantis wants you off the band." John said, matter-of-factly.

Audrey could feel Matt and Tyler stiffen, as if they had looked into Medusa's eyes. Kevin, however, let out a soft snort as if the mere thought of it was a blasphemy.

"I can't disagree with them." John shook his head and walked toward the coffee pot. "You've done nothing but partying and—apparently—get high. They are tired of it and so am I."

This time, Kevin seemed upset by what he heard. He looked around the room, then tilted his head down as a schoolboy being scolded by his basketball coach in front of the team.

"They can't do that. We have a contract." He muttered.

"Yes, we do. Atlantis contracted us to do a job and you're making it impossible."

"Kevin, man. You can't do this anymore. If you get in deep you can't get out," Tyler said.

"It hasn't been that bad," Kevin said.

"I had to pick you up twice for rehearsal, other times you've been late or drunk—" Matt said.

"Okay, okay. I'm sorry." Kevin rubbed his pale face. "I've messed up. But it's over. I can do this, I'll get it straight."

"You might need...professional help," Audrey said.

"No. I don't need it. Trust me."

Audrey took his words with a great deal of pragmatism, but neither she or the band could force him into rehab if he didn't want to.

Chapter 19

"Oh, John. I'm not going." It was like Audrey had thrown a bucket of cold water at him that day. He met her for lunch in a deli near the darkroom because he couldn't wait to share the good news. They were going to perform at Lake Tahoe Fall's Festival.

"Not going? What do you mean?" Surprised, John froze with his sandwich midair.

"I'm sorry, baby. There is no reason for me to go."

"I'm the reason."

"John . . . I can't follow you around like that. It's ridiculous."

"What I think is ridiculous is us having to be apart because it doesn't seem right to other people." He took a bite of his sandwich.

"Well, it is not just that. I mean, you'll be working. It is a huge deal. You guys have to give it one hundred per cent."

"Last time you were around I think I did pretty well."

Audrey blushed.

"I don't want to leave you alone." John said, soberly.

She knew what he meant; she didn't want to be alone either. The bruises on her body were disappearing, but the image of what had happened remained clear in her head. She'd told John she was fine, but her nightmares told him otherwise. She'd scream in the dark of their bedroom and he'd quickly embrace her and whisper her back to sleep, telling her it was only a bad dream, that he was there and she was okay.

"I can't go, anyway. I haven't finished the work for the show and I'm running behind." She stayed home for a few days after the incident at Ryan Correll's party while John helped Matt and Tyler move Kevin to their apartment—the alternative to rehab.

"I guess you're right." John sounded defeated. "It just seems everything we do keep us apart."

"It seems like that because we've started from the confinement of a Winnebago, anything beyond that compares to. . . ." Audrey looked around the deli searching in vain for the right analogy. "Infinity."

*

When she arrived home that evening, exhausted from the long hours inside the darkroom, John was already there.

"I have a surprise for you." John said.

"Really? What is it?"

"Look what I found." He nodded toward their kitchen table, where a fruit basket was filled with several pieces of fruit.

"Mangos! Where did you get them?" Audrey said.

"I went to the Farmer's Market on Fairfax after lunch."

"John . . ." Audrey grabbed a mango and held it close to her face, closing her eyes and inhaling its sweet scent. "Thank you."

"Look at the label."

She twisted the fruit around until she found the small yellow sticker. "It's from Brazil."

"They could have come from your grandfather's farm."

"Yeah, I guess they could've."

"We could go visit after the touring for this CD is over."

"Can you do that?"

"If Atlantis signs us for a second album, I suppose we'll have some time before we start recording. I'd love to meet your family."

Audrey chuckled. "Careful with what you wish for. They're a crazy bunch. I mean…it has been so long. I only know what my mother tells me about them now."

John ambled up behind her, hugging her waist. "Maybe it has been too long."

"Maybe you're right. I resented my mother for so long for trying to make me more Brazilian. I already felt like an outsider as it was, I didn't need her constant reprimands reminding me I wasn't as American as my peers."

"You're not."

144

Audrey turned to face him.

"You're not like any other woman I've ever met. You're strong and don't take anything for granted. You don't feel entitled to things like other people do."

"But that has nothing to do with being American, It was the way I was raised: to believe you're the only one who can change your own life. It's up to you...well, and God, but that's a different story."

"And who raised you to be like that, your Brazilian mother?" He smiled.

She walked to the counter and sat the mango beside the sink. "I'll make us some salad."

John followed her. "Audrey, there's nothing wrong with being angry at our parents sometimes, but they're just people, like us; they make mistakes."

"I'm not angry at her, anymore. I think I'm...embarrassed. She had it hard when she came to the U.S., barely speaking English and having no money. Living in the very conservative, very white North Shore."

"She must have suffered all kinds of prejudice."

"Oh, yeah. For a while people said that the old guy she was taking care of was her lover. The guy was eighty! Everyone alienated her. And still, she was proud of her heritage and tried to impart it to me, but I behaved like a spoiled brat." Audrey sighed. "I was ashamed of her."

"Your mother loves you very much and she's proud of you." He held her face in his hands.

"Yeah?" Audrey muttered without conviction.

"Of course." He kissed her. "You—liking it or not—are very Brazilian, everyone can see it. And I love it."

Chapter 20

This is unusual, Audrey thought, when Janice told her Edward wanted to see her right away. Most days he was so busy, they barely talked. She knocked on the door of his office, a frosted glass cubicle in a far corner of the studio.

"Audrey, come in. How are you?"

"Doing well. You?"

"Running like a headless chicken. *Vogue* called this morning and they need an emergency photo shoot to run with an article on the selling of Prêt-à-porter—the eBay of fashion couture. Charlie and Ethan are taking over other clients. Can you come to New York with me tonight? We should be back in two days."

"Of course."

Edward told her what to get from the studio and sent her home to pack. She needed to be at LAX at six, which meant leaving much earlier to avoid rush-hour traffic on the 405.

On the way home she texted John, GOING TO NEW YORK WITH EDWARD. BACK IN A COUPLE OF DAYS. LEAVING AT 6. LOVE YOU.

"Hi." The phone rang almost immediately after she'd sent the message.

"Hi babe, what's going on?"

"*Vogue* called, and when they call, you answer it."

"I see."

"The other assistants are busy, and Edward's asked me to help."

"Can you come by Atlantis? I wanted to see you before you go."

"I can't. I am going home to pack, then right back to LAX before traffic gets bad."

"Hmm. Call me when you get there?"

"Will do, honey."

"I love you."

"I love you, too."

*

The photo shoot in New York was like running a marathon. Edward had to improvise because he didn't have everything he was used to working with, including Charlie who intuitively was able to provide Edward with what he needed before he asked. Heck, before he even knew what he wanted, but she, working as if she'd split herself in multiples, did reasonably well. Only when it was over, she had time to appreciate the 360-degrees view of Manhattan from the penthouse *Vogue* had rented. She walked around the perimeter of the glass wall which kept people safely away from the edge of the building. An immaculate rooftop pool was the backdrop for the shoot, where models sat in stylish pool-side chairs dipping their feet in the water and drinking fake martinis while pretending to held joyful conversations. Prêt-à-porter's founder and CEO, a forty-something slim brunette who towered over them wearing a grey dress and Manolos, looked better than any of the models. One of the models had told Audrey it was the same pool where Samantha from *Sex and the City* had skinny-dipped with a boyfriend in the middle of the night, and Audrey imagined John's long body gliding under the blue water and the subdued heat of their bodies keeping them warm.

"Let's pack up and go. We need drinks." Edward met her staring southwest.

"Can you believe it has been ten years?" She looked at the void where the Twin Towers once stood.

"Hard to believe." He nodded.

"This is only the third time I came to New York after it happened. I'm not used to not seeing them there. Were you here?"

"No, I was in London for Labor Day."

"I was in high school. I remember parents coming in crying, picking up their kids, and being afraid the world was going to end."

"It kind of did . . . for Americans, anyway."

Audrey faced him inquisitively.

"Before, they heard about the bad in the world but it was this invisible thing, something that could be easily ignored. Sure, there was Vietnam and Pearl Harbor, but that was war. You kind of expected the worse." Edward faced her, his solemn face beautifully adorned by creases of time. "Americans never had to face the atrocities that happen to good people on a daily basis in some of the other countries. Everyone was so busy. Mortgages. SUVs. Little Leagues."

He turned back to the faint beams of light in the darkening sky. "When September 11th happened, it all became real, tangible. The fire, the bodies, the ashes. Suddenly, life as they'd known it wasn't safe anymore. They joined in the party, all the suffering, and pain, and injustice, and cruelty beyond words."

*

Vogue's designated assistant took Edward's equipment back to Times Square, while Edward and Audrey headed straight to dinner, both starved. The caterers for the shoot weren't bad, but it was one thing eating cold cuts while working, and something else entirely to wind down after a long day in front of a nice hot plate of food and a drink. Edward wanted to go to City Crab, so they walked the twelve-block stretch to 4th Avenue.

"I think you should start making special requests to these magazines. Why have all this status if you can't even eat what you like?" Audrey said.

"I could be Edward: the diva photographer."

"I bet you'd be popular with the models; their newest BFF."

"BFF?"

"Best Friend Forever."

"Are you taking the piss?" He snorted. "What are you, sixteen?"

"What are you, one hundred?

"I feel like one hundred right now. Thank you for that."

"Sorry. Don't you talk to the models at all? I mean, you'll learn all kinds of things. You shouldn't pass up the opportunity."

"I think I hear a judgmental tone in your voice. Besides, I'd rather date them."

She thought of at least one joke she could have made right then, but she was suddenly quiet. They strode the streets coated by dark and the pre-autumn air cleared away summer's mugginess.

"Well, at least I used to. Now they're getting younger and younger, and I've grown older and older." Edward rubbed his shaved head and chin, where stubs of gray hair peaked out from his black skin.

"Don't feel bad, grandpa. You still got it." Audrey wasn't lying. Edward was sculpted like a totemic panther, tall and athletic with narrow black eyes and full lips.

"How old are you, Audrey?"

"Twenty-eight."

Edward's smile was nostalgic. "I am forty-eight."

"*O tempo não para não,*" Audrey said, half to herself.

"Is it Portuguese? What does it mean?"

"Yes. It means: time doesn't stop. It's from one of my mom's favorite Brazilian musicians."

Around eleven, they left City Crab stuffed, tipsy, and happy. Edward was fun to hang out with; in L.A. he was so busy, she had never known that side of him. He said his girlfriend of four years had broken up with him not long ago. She was a writer and had taken a job in New York—to get away from him. Being in the city brought up feelings he'd tried to ignore.

"What is it that makes one fall out of love?" he asked when they sat at the bar in the Bulldog's Pub.

Audrey stared into her Guinness; she couldn't answer him. She had fallen out of love with an ex-boyfriend without knowing how it happened. She wondered if at some point he'd asked the same question to someone, somewhere.

"I understand when there are arguments, fights. . . ." He gulped his own Guinness. "Bad sex. We had none of that, it was great. We got along. I loved . . . love . . . her." He looked at himself in the mirror behind the bar, a bottle of Jack Daniels over half of his face.

Audrey tried to think how to change the subject quickly; he seemed about to start crying.

"I wish I had seen the signs." He finished his Guinness and ordered them another round along with Jägermeister shots. "There must have been signs." He knocked down his shot and slammed the cup on the worn dark wood bar.

"Have you talked to her since?" She was going down a dark path, but she had to say something. Perhaps talking about it would help him get over and move on.

"She called me on my birthday." Edward nodded, smiling.

"Sometimes when you don't have something is when you realize you need it." For an instant, she felt a little preachy, but the last shot of Jägermeister had gone right to her head and the words came out of her mouth big and fluffy.

"She doesn't know I'm here, so maybe I should call her." He looked at Audrey, his eyes wide and sparkly. "Should I call her?"

Oh, crap. She hated giving advice, especially love advice. She knocked down her Guinness and took her time savoring the rich dark liquid running down her throat, but he was still waiting. "What do you want to do?"

"I think it looks very indifferent to come all the way to New York and not even let her know I was here." He ordered more shots with a wave of his fingers.

"Edward, calling her is like jumping off a plane without—absolute certainty—your parachute is going to open."

They clicked their glasses and downed the shots.

"All right." He pulled his cell out of his pocket.

"I'm going to the bathroom." She climbed off her stool and pulled her own cell from her messenger bag. She had missed a call—John's.

"Hey babe." He answered when she called him back.

"Hi, I've missed your call." She leaned against a corner in the hallway that led to the restrooms, covering her ear with one hand and heard his voice.

"How's it going?"

"Great, we've finished the photo shoot today. We're in a pub right now, Edward is hammered."

"And you?"

"Not at all." Audrey could hear John's muffled laughter. "I'm serious."

"Just don't miss your plane tomorrow. I miss you."

"You know I won't, I miss you too. Besides I think I'm done for the night, Edward is calling his ex right now. I'll take a cab to the hotel."

"Okay, call me tomorrow from the airport."

She walked into the bathroom and washed her face. She was drunk, she could see it in her bloodshot eyes and flushed skin. When she got back, Edward looked like he was hunched over his glass holding the weight of his head with his hands, elbows propped on the bar. Rodin's *The Thinker* couldn't have looked more somber.

She placed a hand on his shoulder. "What happened?"

"She is with someone else."

"Did she say that?"

"She didn't have to. I heard him. I could hear it in her voice."

"Edward, I'm sorry." She rubbed his shoulder and looked at the glasses in front of him; he had had at least a couple more shots before she got back.

He clicked his tongue and said, "My parachute didn't open."

*

It was three in the morning when she helped him to his room. He'd talked about his ex-girlfriend all night—except when dancing.

He looked like a giant marionette with arms pumping and legs kicking, as if his strings were worked by a madman. She'd been torn—laughing at Edward's spasmodic routine on the dance floor and distressed over his cries at the table.

Inside his room, he flopped on the bed. She offered him water, he only groaned. She pulled his shoes off and turned around to leave, but he held her wrist and stood.

"Audrey, you're a good friend." He hugged her.

"You too, Edward."

He brushed his face against hers, placed his hands on her neck and, before she could realize what he was doing, his tongue fumbled into her mouth. His hands traveled down and squeezed the small of her back. For a split second, it felt nice: heat, and his saliva, and alcohol. John. It wasn't John.

"No." She pushed Edward back on the bed. Adrenaline, like a dull knife, had cut her brain into pieces of aching tissue. The pain was so acute she had to massage her eyes with her fingers.

"Audrey, I'm sorry." His voice faded as she slammed the door behind her.

She was in tears when she arrived at her own room, two floors up. Desolation—and probably alcohol—numbed her body as if she had slid through broken ice and fallen into a frozen lake. It never crossed her mind that a kiss between two drunks was too silly of a thing to mention. How could she keep a secret—any secret—from John for the rest of her life?

"Hello?" John muttered, half asleep.

"It's me."

"Hi babe, what time is it?"

She swallowed a sob.

"Are you okay? What's going on?"

"We kissed."

"What? What are you talking about?"

"I helped Edward to his room because he was so wasted. He

said I'm a good friend, because I had listened to him talking about his ex all night. He'd hugged me and before I knew it, we were kissing."

Dead silence.

"It didn't last ten seconds, it meant nothing." It was possible she was drunker than she thought because she couldn't hold the sobs. "Please say something."

"I thought you were going to the hotel four hours ago."

"I was. Edward was upset because his ex-girlfriend was with another guy when he called her." She swiped the tears and snot that collapsed down her face away with her forearm.

"So, he wanted you to be his rebound?"

"It wasn't like that. He is so drunk I don't think he even knows who I am."

There was a long pause. She could hear her own fear pulsing through her body.

"John, you know me. I love you."

Silence. Someone must have pressed the freeze-frame, because the whole world stood still.

"I don't know what else to say."

"There's nothing else to say, Audrey. I don't want to talk anymore. Go to sleep, it sounds like you need it."

*

At almost check-out time, she got a text from Edward, I HAD TO STOP BY VOGUE. SEE YOU AT THE AIRPORT.

At least one piece of good news: she wouldn't have to see Edward so soon. She thought about changing flights, but it would be a hassle; she'd have to face him sooner or later.

He showed up at the gate almost at boarding time, took an empty seat beside hers, and opened a bottle of water.

"Here, I got you one."

"No, thanks."

"Hey, did we kiss last night?"

Didn't he remember? "You kissed me."

"Damn, I wasn't dreaming." He took a long pull of water and said, "So, how was it?"

"Terrible."

He chuckled. "I wasn't playing my A game."

If she had had a gun, the police would have had to mop up his head off the floor.

"I told John. He was upset, and he didn't want to talk to me. I tried to call him today—" She was staring at the phone, clasped in her hands. "He won't answer."

"I'm so sorry. I shouldn't be joking. Honestly, I wasn't sure it happened." He placed his hand on hers, but she recoiled. "I can talk to John. I'll tell him it was stupid, I was plastered—"

"I don't think it will help. John doesn't open up to everyone. You really have to earn his trust and I've lost it." She said, half to herself, "I'm not sure I can get it back."

Chapter 21

Audrey came home to an empty house. John still wouldn't return her calls. She let her bag drop to the floor, and walked through the house, still hoping to find him, but in the bedroom there was only a note on the bed.

> *I need time to think.*
> *I will be at Matt's.*
> *J.*

She grabbed the phone from her bag, and texted him: just got home, saw your note. sorry you feel this way. i'll be here. love you. Then, she showered and went to bed. Hours later the bell rang. She thought she was still asleep, but it rang again. John? She jumped out of bed and ran to the door, but remembered he had a key. It was Matt, and without saying a word, he stepped in and opened his arms.

She burrowed her face into his chest and said, "Matt, I screwed up."

"Hush now." Matt stroked her hair. "He is upset, but he'll get over it."

"I don't know how it happened. I never meant for it to happen."

"I know. Come on, let's have a beer." He led her to the kitchen.

"Oh, no. No beer for me." She rubbed her head.

"Okay, beer for me, tea for you."

They talked for a long time. John had already told him about the kiss, but she narrated what had happened again, almost word by word, including that Edward didn't even remember kissing her.

"What I don't get is, why did you even tell John?" Matt propped his feet on the coffee table.

Audrey sipped at her tea. "I'll never keep anything from him, no matter how small," she said, very quietly.

"Fair enough."

"Will he forgive me?

"Of course he will."

"When?" She looked at him eagerly as if he was about to tell her how long she had to live.

"Just give the butt-head time to digest. He's scared, that's all."

"No, he trusted me. I've messed up. I should have gone back to the hotel when I said I would."

"And leave your friend alone feeling like shit? Not the Audrey I know."

Her face showed the faintest trace of a smile. "I wish he would see it like you do."

Matt placed his bottle on the coffee table. "I've known John since before his mother's death, they were really close. He's always been quiet, but after . . . uh, he sort of built this wall around him. I guess he thought if no one got close enough he wouldn't have to deal with losing anyone again. But you got in. He just doesn't know how to handle it yet."

Audrey muttered, "He should at least stay in his house. I can stay somewhere else."

"This is your house, too. Besides, give him a couple of days on our couch and he'll come crawling back."

*

Given a choice, she would have chosen to stay in bed until John came back. Her night had been restless, unsure if she was awake, dreaming, or sleepwalking in the dark looking for him, feeling his presence in the pitch-black, but finding no walls to pat, no light seeping through to guide her in any direction, only emptiness.

The group show was less than a month away, so she had to get up. She got her camera and left to scout locations. She'd taken the "ghost pictures," as Charlie had baptized them, in Silver Lake, Echo Park, and downtown, and she wanted check out South L.A.

It was hard to spend the entire day without talking to John, but she pretended he was on a gig out of town.

Had she just now realized how much she needed him? The same way she'd preached to Edward about people who realize what they need only after they lost it. Had she lost John? No, impossible. They knew how much they meant to each other. Didn't they? Were there signs? Could John have fallen out of love because of her stupid mistake? Those thoughts raced through her head all day. It was hard to work, but she took enough photographs to keep her in the darkroom the rest of the week.

Matt had told her the band was going to play in the Lake Tahoe's Fall Festival next week. Rob had returned from summer vacation with his daughter, and was coming back to drive the new tour bus. Atlantis had other drivers, but John insisted. She was happy Rob was coming back, but sad this time—more than likely—she wouldn't be in the bus with them. The band was leaving the day after tomorrow. She hoped John would talk to her before then.

When she was heading home, Megan called to check on her. It turned out that Edward had told Charlie who told Megan. Audrey didn't want to talk about it anymore; she wanted to forget it ever happened, but apparently, that wasn't an option.

"What are you going to do?" Megan asked

"What can I do? He won't talk to me."

"It sounds like he's never been drunk enough to do something stupid."

"It's a little more complicated than that."

"Is it really? You weren't the one who kissed in the first place."

She let out a big sigh, not wanting to think about what she felt when Edward kissed her, that one second she gave in to raw desire before she remembered it wasn't John's lips on hers. She couldn't forgive herself and it was probably why John couldn't, either.

"Why don't you come over? I can make us something to eat and we can talk."

"No, thanks. I want to be home in case he shows up. He's going on a trip in a couple of days, and he'll need to pack." Audrey felt a twitch of embarrassment, but if that was the only way she was going to see him, she'd gladly take it.

"Hey, don't beat yourself too hard, girl. Men are dumb; it can take them awhile."

"Girls can be dumb, too."

*

Late at night, she sat at her kitchen table studying her contact sheets and using a silver marker to circle the images she intended to print. The challenge was to edit them down; she already had too many and still had three rolls of negatives to develop. Ben was going to help her choose in order to keep the show cohesive. Normally, she would have shown them to Edward first, but that was out of the question now. She didn't want to get near him before she straightened things out with John.

Every other thought she had was about him. By now, Matt would have told him about their conversation. She hoped Matt would get through him, but knowing John he wouldn't even listen.

Fuck it. She grabbed her car keys and walked out. Ten minutes later, Tyler opened the door of his apartment.

"Audrey," He seemed surprised.

"Hi Tyler."

"What's going on?"

"I need to talk to John. Is he here?"

"Hey, Audrey," Matt, punching his fingers on a XBOX remote, greeted her without without taking his eyes off the TV. "He is in my room."

Audrey swallowed hard and walked into the apartment. She opened the bedroom door. John was stretched out on the bed with one hand behind his head and the other holding his cell.

"What are you doing here?" He sat up.

"We need to talk." She stepped in and closed the door behind her. "You wouldn't answer my calls."

"I need some time," he said, walking toward the window.

"Time for what, John? I didn't devise a plan to hurt you or to cheat on you. I was drunk and a guy kissed me. I pushed him off and walked away."

"You put yourself in that position," he said, looking out the window and rubbing his head, distraught.

"Position? I was out with my boss. I didn't go out randomly looking for trouble." She took a tentative step forward. "A few months ago you told me you didn't want to spend a second apart from me, now you won't even take my calls. Which one is it?"

"I am upset."

"I know you are and it's killing me. But I love you. I love you. Don't you believe that?"

"I thought the only thing no one could ever take from me was you. Nothing could change what we had, no matter how strange or complicated this life got. I was wrong."

"I am yours and nothing will change that."

"Everything has changed."

"What are you talking about?"

They stood for a moment in silence, she had a vague sense something else was bothering him.

"Atlantis wants to replace Kevin," he said sulkily.

"What?"

He turned from the window to face her and said, "He showed up drunk at the studio a few times and after his accident, they think he is a liability. It's either Kevin or the second album."

"John, I'm sorry. Have you told Tyler and Matt?"

He shook his head.

"Let me be with you." Audrey stepped closer, but he retreated, her heart sank and her voice softened. "You don't have to do it alone."

"I can't risk it. It hurts too much."

"What are you saying? Is . . . is it over?"

He lowered his head mournfully and closed his eyes. "I don't know."

Audrey stepped back until she hit the door, glad to have something to hold her up. She felt as if the ground had just cracked open under her feet.

She wanted to beg him, she wanted to turn back time, she wanted to die, but instead she inhaled deeply and said, "I know you need to get ready for your trip. You don't need to sleep on a couch anymore. I'll be out of your house tomorrow." She opened the door and marched out, flying by Matt and Tyler without a word.

Chapter 22

"Of course, you can stay with me. It will be great." Megan sounded incredibly excited about having a fourth person in her small two-bedroom apartment.

"Just for a few days. Until I figure out my next move," Audrey told her on the phone while throwing her bag inside the Prius's tiny trunk, wishing she had picked a SUV.

"Your next move? John will come to his senses before you unpack."

"You know what? He might, he might not, but I'm not going to sit around and wait."

"What's with the new skeptical Audrey?"

Audrey took one last look at the living room before she closed the door, dried-eye and tired. "She's not new, she's just back."

*

The band had left for Utah, but not a word from John. She imagined he'd been feeling what she'd started to feel—betrayed.

Kevin was the one who called from the road, but she wished he hadn't. She planned to keep her mind completely occupied with the preparations for her show, and, thus far, it had worked, more or less. Every time her thoughts wandered, she focused on a different print to make.

"Why am I always the last one to know?" Kevin said.

"Sorry, forgot to include your email address in my newsletter's roster." She set the darkroom's timer for ten minutes, and looked at the freshly developed photographs rocking slowly inside the washer, remembering what John had said about Atlantis's demand to have Kevin off the band.

"Seriously, you're making our lives miserable. He's been such a sourpuss."

"Kevin, please, I don't want to talk about him." Her voice shrieked around "him," as if thinking of his name hurt like a pinched nerve. She grabbed a cigarette from her purse and walked out of the darkroom. Smoking made her feel nauseated, but she wanted to feel something besides what she actually did. "How's the festival?"

"All right. Some of these bands are pretty good. Can't wait to get back to L.A., though."

It was hard to believe what a jerk Kevin had transformed into since becoming famous. Less than six months ago, the band would not have been hired to play in such a large event; now, he made it sound like it was beneath him.

"Los Angeles will dismiss you as quickly as you do the poor girls you trick into sleeping with you."

"God, I've missed you."

"Seriously Kevin, get a grip, will you? Who do you think you are, Mick Jagger?"

"I could be."

"Remember your career has just started. You have one CD, a couple hits, and a drinking problem. Hardly enough for one hour of True Hollywood Stories."

"Aw, I know now who's the sourpuss."

Impossible. What does it take to get through this thick head? Her cigarette had burned down to a stub. She crushed it out and moved toward the door. "Kevin, I have to go."

"Okay, I guess I'll have to make do with Jennifer?"

Jennifer?

*

The song "Wonderful Woman" woke her the next morning. It was the ringtone she'd chosen for her dad. As a teenager, The Smiths had brought them together, as his image of old and boring had changed favorably when she'd found out he liked them.

She tapped the floor beside her blow-up mattress searching for the phone without fully opening her eyes. "Hi Dad."

"It's Mom. I forgot my phone in the house."

"Hi Mom."

"How are you, sweetie?"

"Sleepy."

"Still?"

"What time is it?"

"It's, uh, Pacific time . . . seven. Oh, sorry. I keep forgetting."

"That's fine, Mom. What's up?" Audrey propped herself on her elbow to look at Megan's bed: empty.

"We're at the mall. Would John like a grill set?"

"Uh?" Audrey only heard "John."

"Spatula, corn holders, aluminum storage case—"

"Mom, what are you talking about?"

"Your father and I would like to get him something for when we get there. For the house."

Audrey sighed heavily and stretched onto the mattress again, her hand covering her face. She'd wanted to delay telling her parents about the situation between she and John as long as possible, hoping things would have been sorted out before they came to L.A. for the show.

She swallowed hard, feeling her throat sore and dry, and said, "Mom, John and I broke up." In all the days they had been apart, she dreaded the word "break-up." They hadn't broken up; he'd said "I don't know," nothing more. But at that moment, she couldn't think of a simpler way to put it.

There was a silence, just long enough for Audrey's negligible amount of disposition to wilt.

"Oh, sweetie. What happened?"

"Long story. I'd rather not talk about it."

"I'm sorry," Isabel whispered, then said more tenderly, "Real love never fails. Sometimes it breaks, but the mended pieces become stronger than before."

"Or it will never be the same."

"Shh—you'll be all right."

"You and Dad will have to stay in a hotel," Audrey said, very quietly.

"Where are you staying?"

"With a friend. Her name is Megan. You'll meet her."

"How long has it been?"

"Almost a week."

"Audrey,"—Isabel sounded upset.—"you have been living with a stranger for a week and haven't even bothered to tell us."

"She's not a stranger, and I've been a little preoccupied with the show."

"It doesn't matter. I bet she doesn't even know our telephone number. If something happens to you, she couldn't contact us."

"Mom, bad news travel fast—"

"Apparently not."

"Besides, she knows Matt."

"Oh, how's Matt?" Isabel asked cheerily.

"Peachy," Audrey said, with feigned indignation.

"How's work for the show?"

"Coming along."

"And at the studio?"

"Not doing that anymore."

"Really? What happened there?"

"Uh. . . ."

"Let me guess, it's complicated."

Audrey couldn't help but chuckle, her mother had developed such a lightness with age, it made her want to be curled up on her mother's lap. For sure, Isabel wasn't the same mother she had growing up, always pushing her to do more, do better, be someone exceptional. Perhaps Isabel had given up already. Good. Or she finally realized that Audrey wasn't her second chance to accomplish the things she never had. For a while, Audrey hoped that if she ever got pregnant she would have a boy. So there would be no risk of transferring her unfulfilled dreams to the poor soul who hadn't even asked to be born.

*

Audrey wished the darkroom she'd rented was like a 24-Hour Fitness. She hoped for a key to get in at any time of day or night. She didn't want stop working, even when her feet throbbed from the droned hours spent pulling sheets of fiber paper from developer, to fixer, to stop bath, and to the wash. Instead, she had to stop at 9:45 p.m. to clean up and leave by ten when the front desk tech would knock on the door. She tried to talk him into letting her stay, but the poor guy must have had a life, because he'd snorted with incredulity as if she had asked him for money.

"I can lock up. No one will even know I'm here," Audrey pleaded.

"It's against the rules. I'll be in trouble if Jason finds out." He shook his head.

Jason must have been the owner. She hated Jason.

Staying with Megan had become torture, since she seemed to have made cheering Audrey up her mission in life. Megan's perkiness grew proportionally with Audrey's gloominess, transforming their exchanges into a rehearsal for a tragi-comic off-Broadway play.

"Hey, dude," Megan said cheerfully, when Audrey opened the door of her room.

Megan made it impossible for Audrey to crawl under the covers of the blow-up mattress and shut the world out. She didn't want to stay awake, her brain torturing her with thoughts of John. His absence was palpable and it hurt like an open wound. All she wanted was to float above consciousness where they were still together. She dreamt of him every night, cooking in their bungalow, or making love on the floor, or sitting on the bench in their backyard watching the sunlight being swallowed by dusk.

"Hi." Dude?

"Where have you been all day?"

"In the darkroom."

"Until midnight?"

"Oh, no. Ten. I drove around a bit." When Audrey drove by an In-N-Out Burger, her stomach reminded her the last time she ate was breakfast. Instead of turning around, she drove aimlessly, zigzagging street blocks like a game of PAC-MAN, until she found another.

"Guess where we're going tomorrow, dude?"

"To a Justin Timberlake concert?" Audrey said wryly.

"To the beach."

"Beach?"

"Uh-huh, Malibu. Charlie is taking us surfing."

"Oh." Audrey had told Megan only a couple of days earlier how much she enjoyed surfing in Japan. This wasn't a coincidence. "I have to work tomorrow."

"Oh, no." Megan, sitting cross legged on her bed, placed her fists on her hips. "The darkroom is open only for four hours on Saturdays. You can make it up next week by working until midnight again."

"Ten." It dawned on Audrey she was being a little ungracious, Megan had obviously put some work into this outing by mobilizing Charlie. "Okay."

*

The day was overcast and the ocean was calm, and at that time in the morning it kept the— rightly named—Surfrider beach in Malibu empty. Audrey sat on her rented surfboard rocking on the ocean—a baby cradled in maternal arms. She was, supposedly, waiting for a good wave, but had missed several in the thirty minutes she'd been there. She imagined herself as a beach marker buoy, dividing the shore from the dangerous depths of the unknown. She looked out to where the ocean met the sky, smooth and heavy as a piece of slate against an airy pale blue wall, and started to paddled toward it, hoping to go on forever until she disappeared. Salty droplets of water splashed onto her face as her arms circled around to move her forward. At a distance, she saw the ocean rising as if it had been just awaken from sleep. A wave formed like a crease in a wool blanket. As a surge of adrenaline pumped through her body, she forgot her intentions to vanish between water and air and turned her board around. She paddled, looking over her shoulder, studying the wave to discover where exactly it would burst into the ticklish flakes that would take her back to shore. To reality. Then she strengthened her grip, stiffened her spine and, in a quick motion, curled her legs onto the board. When she found her center of gravity, she opened her hands and carefully balanced herself up. Riding the wave as if it was a wild stallion ready to throw her off, all of her sadness disappeared under the sounds of her throbbing pulse in her ears and the sizzling of the water under her feet. She closed her eyes. The next instant, she was inside the water swimming toward the surface with the safety strap of the board tugging at her ankle.

Chapter 23

"No, you keep it." Edward pushed back the camera bag Audrey placed on his desk. "I'm glad it's been put to good use again."

"Edward, if wasn't for you, this show wouldn't be happening. I'll be forever grateful." She handed him a postcard for the opening, suspecting he wouldn't come if she didn't invite him in person.

"Maybe not at Ben's gallery, but somewhere else. He should be the one thanking me." He looked up at her and smiled. "What is it you're going to do next?"

"Continue working. Photographing."

"Good for you," he said, putting the invitation on his desk and sighing deeply. "Look, Audrey, I'm very sorry for the problem I've caused between you and John. It's by far one of the stupidest things I've ever done, but I need you to know I never meant to hurt you."

"I know that, Edward."

"Forgive me for saying, but that bloke is an obstinate bastard."

"He has a lot on his mind. The issue is way deeper than the kiss, you shouldn't worry about it." She smiled wryly and said, "You're off the hook."

"When my girlfriend broke up with me out of the blue—at least I thought it was." He nodded at Audrey with pensive eyes. "I was pretty shaken, thought I wouldn't recover." Then, he said with a reassuring smile, "But, eventually, you make a choice…to keep going…to be happy again. You'll recover, give it time."

"I don't have a choice, Edward. I couldn't forget him even if I wanted to."

He took in what she'd said, clicked his tongue, and apologized again and again.

It didn't matter anymore.

*

"Red light." Audrey said from inside the darkroom as someone knocked on the door.

"Audrey, it's me. We need to talk." Megan said.

What is she doing here? Audrey thought. Geez, more cheering up already? Just kill me now. "Just a second." She pulled a test print from the developer and threw it into the stop bath, then, making sure there was no paper exposed, turned on the light and opened the door.

Megan, walking into the ten-by-ten room, glanced at the stained sink, the rack of prints on the corner, the trays of chemicals along a wall and said, "How can you stand this all day, in the dark?"

Audrey looked around and said, "It feels like home to me."

"Can we go get some coffee?" Megan shriveled.

"I have tons of work—"

"It's important."

"Fine, but I can't take long. There's a coffee shop two blocks down."

Audrey and Megan both ordered Thai lattes and sat at a table on the corner.

"Can you please just tell me what's going on? Are you kicking me out?"

"Don't be silly." Megan rolled her eyes.

"What then?"

Megan opened her purse and pulled out a magazine from it. "I'm sorry to show you this, but I thought it might be easier coming from a friend."

It was a copy of *OK!* with a distraught Lindsay Lohan on the cover, and on the bottom right corner, just above the barcode was John and Jennifer, sitting together at a bar: him smiling, her leaning toward him with her hand on his thigh. The caption above the picture: "North Star's Supernova, hot guitarist hook up in Lake Tahoe."

"Audrey, this doesn't mean anything. For all we know, this bitch sent this picture to the paparazzi herself."

Audrey grabbed the magazine, thumbing the pages hurriedly, looking for more information. There was nothing much inside the magazine about the photo, just a recap on how the band came to stardom, an old picture of John and Audrey together somewhere she couldn't even remember, a detail of Jennifer from the picture on the cover, and the rhetorical question: Has he found another muse?

"She went to Lake Tahoe with them . . . on the bus." Audrey mumbled.

"I'm sorry, hon." Megan said softly and, when Audrey remained motionless and pale as a ghost, she said "Look, today is Tuesday; they are back, aren't they? This picture is from Friday. Call him and find out the truth."

"I gotta get out of here." Audrey grabbed her bag and stood up, bumping the table and spilling her drink all over the magazine.

"Audrey, wait!"

She ran for one block before tears blinded her. She tripped and fell, scraping her hands and knees on the ground.

"Audrey, my God. Are you okay?"

"It's over, Megan. It's really over." She cried while Megan helped her up.

"Don't be ridiculous. It's a tabloid."

"He was smiling. He looked happy."

"You're a photographer. You know it took a split second to snap that picture, he could have been picking his teeth and we wouldn't know the difference."

"It has been over a week . . . he hasn't called." Audrey's voice trailed off.

When they arrived at the darkroom, Megan said "Let's go home. You shouldn't be inside this cave, alone, all day."

"I have to work. I'm fine. I promise."

"Then, I'll stick around."

"No, really. I do have to finish this print. It's the last one for the show."

Megan looked at Audrey with a disapproving eye.

"I won't kill myself with photography chemicals. I'm fucking devastated, but I'm no moron. It's just a broken heart, right? We've all been there."

"Fine, but if you don't answer you phone I'll be back—with Charlie."

"Don't worry."

Megan gave her a hug and left. Audrey closed the door, slid down to the floor, and cried for hours.

*

"Audrey." John came out of his car as she approached the Prius in the parking lot at the end of the day.

"John, what are you doing here?"

"I have to talk to you."

"About you and Jennifer? Spare me, I already know."

"That's why I came, there's nothing to know."

"Do you mean she wasn't in the tour bus with you? You weren't partying in Lake Tahoe? That photograph was never taken? You didn't break up with me over a week ago?"

"Audrey, I'm sorry."

"For what? Any or all of the above?"

"I'm sorry I've put you through this—all of it. Since we've been together, I'd never thought about the possibility of losing you. After you called me from New York. . . . It was like waking up from a dream and discovering I was still inside a nightmare."

"You didn't lose me. You let me go."

"I was a coward . . . insecure. I've made a mistake."

"So, now that you've paid me back, you changed your mind?"

"No! Nothing happened between me and Jennifer. She showed up the day we left and announced she was coming with us. We were all at a restaurant when someone took that picture. I was laughing at Matt goofing around."

"It doesn't matter. It's better this way. We're different, we're going different places. If "North Star" hadn't become a hit, who knows. We probably wouldn't have stayed together as long as we did."

"That's bullshit, Audrey. And you know it." He stepped closer and reached for her, but as soon as his fingertips brushed her face, she moved away. "I love you. I will love you forever."

"You were right, John. It hurts too much." She got in the car and drove away.

Chapter 24

Soon the opening reception for the show was upon her.

"Honey, go to work, don't worry about us. We'll see you there." Her mom hugged and kissed her for the thirtieth time since they arrived.

"Okay, then. Ben wants all the artists to come early and I still have to go get ready." She had picked her parents up at LAX and took them to a hotel in West Hollywood.

"Sweetie, I think we should have dinner tomorrow. Tonight it will be too crazy and I'm already tired from the flight." Her dad had already lain down on the bed.

"Oh, Dad. I want to take you guys to a Brazilian place I went with—" She stopped herself and turned to her mom. "It's really good, mom."

"Is John coming tonight? I would really like to meet the young man," her father said.

"George." Isabel, standing by the edge of the bed, slapped his foot.

"It might be a little late for that, Dad."

She went to Megan's apartment to get ready. The couple of days she had intended to crash there had turned into weeks. But that night, the storm would blow over. There was nothing she could do about John and whatever she could have done to put up a strong exhibition she did. Dodging. Burning. Reprinting. She took Ben's suggestion to sepia-tint a few images, and create triptychs from the photographs she took in South L.A. With his help, she was able to borrow expensive aged wood frames from a shop he'd sent business to over the years. The day before the show, she was overwhelmed with emotion when she saw that Ben had chosen those images for the gallery window. The letters of her name along with those of the other artists, were being stuck to the glass in bold black type. She'd adjusted her eyes to focus on her reflection. She looked for the girl who'd gotten drunk over a lost job she hated, the girl who was so afraid to live that she'd hidden inside a cubicle punching numbers into a black screen. The trade-off didn't look much better; she saw a sad woman who had become a little bitter, empty inside from a heart that was given away. A hollow tree waiting for the wind to topple it down. At least now, she had art. Under the red lights, she could look at the images materializing onto the white paper. She could find meaning and give meaning. She could cry without shedding any tears.

*

She'd decided the reception would be a success; she would smile and talk and drink chilled Chardonnay and humbly express her gratitude for all the praises. Then she would leave. She had nothing else to do in L.A. Her parents wanted to see California: San Diego, Malibu, Santa Barbara, San Francisco, so after she chaperoned them, she was going to drop the Prius at the dealership. Then she planned to take the Amtrak back to Illinois on her own, stopping wherever she wanted to take photographs.

There were heaps of people in the gallery. Audrey was wearing a simple lavender dress and black wedges. Everyone congratulated and petted her, smiling. She smiled back, feeling her face hurt after a while. When Matt and Tyler arrived she was certain John wasn't coming. In a way, it helped her relax and concentrate on the people who came to celebrate with her. She needed to honor their gesture with her full attention. Even Kevin showed up, his nonchalant praises suggesting he didn't have a lot to drink, which truly touched her. Charlie and Matt brought flowers and she held both bouquets in her arms while her friends encircled her with love.

When Audrey and her parents got back to the hotel, John was waiting. She didn't notice him at first, leaning against his car under a dim light in the parking lot.

"Hi," he said, straightening up and rubbing his hands.

Audrey was petrified. The last conversation they had in a parking lot didn't turn out well.

Her mother looked back and forth between Audrey's and John's faces, waiting for her to say something.

"John, it is so nice to see you." Isabel finally walked toward him, giving him a hug and a kiss on the cheek.

He was surprised by her warmth. "You too, Mrs. Whitman."

"Oh please, call me Isabel."

John repeated shyly, "Isabel."

"John, nice to finally meet you," Her dad extended his arm.

"Very nice to meet you, sir."

The exchange seemed as surreal as if she was watching them from outside her body.

"George, let's go inside and let the kids talk." Isabel placed her hand on George's elbow.

Audrey and John stood there for a few seconds looking at each other, unable to speak.

"Congratulations on the show, Matt said it was amazing."

"Why are you here?"

"I called Megan. She told me where you're staying. I wanted to go to the show, but I didn't want to upset you. I'm very proud of you, babe."

"Thanks, that's kind of you. I have to go, the folks are exhausted. I don't want to keep them up." She began to walk away.

His voice dropped to a whisper. "Audrey."

She stopped without turning back. In her dreams, she'd still run to his arms in tears of happiness. Now, in the dark of the night, her eyes were dry and her stomach churned.

"I was so scared. I'm still scared," he said.

Audrey was quiet, her back to him.

"Please, Audrey."

She turned around, and said, "John, I know how scared you

were because it's how I've been since we've got to this Godforsaken city. But. . . ." She took a step closer. "I thought we could see each other through the bullshit. John—" She shook her head slowly.

"I can't do it anymore. I've tried to go on, but there's nowhere to go." John closed the distance between them in three long strides and took her face in his hands. "Please, don't do this to us. You know we belong together."

His touch shook her body the same way a defibrillator's electrical waves reignite a dormant heart. She closed her eyes and breathed in his scent, feeling the warmth of his hands on her skin. She knew in a place deeper than her bones it was true: they belonged together. It could be a curse or a blessing when two people are so right for each other they feel like halves of the same whole. Unable to rationalize any longer, she threw her arms around his neck and kissed him.

Earth tilted back on its axis as they stood there, holding each other for several minutes.

"Can we go home now?" John whispered.

"I was going to stay with my parents." Audrey mumbled.

"We'll be back in the morning and take them to breakfast."

"Okay. Let's go in and tell them."

*

Audrey and John undressed each other slowly and made love on the wrought iron bed they'd chosen for their house. No more beseeching for forgiveness was necessary; their bodies did all the talking, and it was enough to mend the cracks created by the weeks apart.

She woke the next day and found him staring at her.

"Hi." He leaned forward and nuzzled her hair.

They lay sideways, facing each other, and John seemed to study her face like an astronomer looking at the stars.

"What are you thinking?" she asked.

"What would happen if we just walked away?"

"Walked away?"

"Yes. From L.A., from Atlantis."

"From Bill."

"From everyone."

"Get in a tour bus again and travel the country one pub at the time?"

"No, no tour bus. No band, just you and me."

Audrey face stiffened. John was not likely to leave his bandmates. "John . . . What's going on?"

He rolled onto his back. "Kevin was so drunk in Utah that we barely finished the concert. He missed several notes, tripped on stage. It was a mess."

Audrey propped herself onto one elbow and placed her hand on his chest.

"Maybe if he knew his job was at stake, it would straighten him up."

"I've told him all of our jobs are at stake if he doesn't pull himself together."

"But it's not true."

"No. Atlantis will keep the band without Kevin."

"Can't Bill do anything?"

"Bill wants me to take Kevin's place."

"What are you going to do?"

"Fly to Brazil?" He raised his eyebrows and gave her a pleading look.

"How about your music?"

"My music is not mine anymore, remember? We had to 'make it more appealing to a wider market.'"

"They might have added some strings and chorus, but those songs are beautiful and they are all you."

"Next album, it will be worse. Tom, the professional song writer Atlantis is shoving down our throats, wants to turn us into some of the American Idol runner-ups he's worked with." He sighed. "I've never written a song worrying if it would be appealing or become a hit."

She stared at him, wishing she could help somehow. He was like an autumn leaf stuck into an icy sidewalk in the middle of the winter; every time someone walked over it, a thin sliver would tear out until there was nothing left. Yet she feared what might happen if he followed Atlantis's demands to change, as many musicians in similar situations did. Then the band's popularity would be built on a sound that was not their own, making it impossible to change back to what they had been in the first place.

"You have to tell them."

"Except for Kevin getting kicked off the band, they know." He pressed the back of her hand on his lips. "But you know Matt, he can smell roses in a shit storm, Tyler will play whatever, and Kevin, uh, he is on another planet."

Chapter 25

The plans for John's birthday were relayed by Jennifer only the day before the event: the band would finish work in the studio as usual, then go to the rooftop bar at The Standard Hotel for a bogus dinner meeting she made up as an excuse to surprise him. Audrey could show up if she wanted to.

"Tell me again; why is this girl still around your boyfriend?" Megan asked over the phone when Audrey called to invite her.

"Jennifer is a publicist for Atlantis. Technically, she has done nothing wrong, and I'm sure she was told to do something for his birthday." Audrey didn't buy for a second the excuse Jennifer had given John at the VMAs, or her incidental proximity to him in Utah, but she was the band's publicist and there was nothing Audrey could do to keep her away from him.

"I still think it's infuriating."

"I didn't know you had the jealousy bug in you. It must be that hot Southern temper."

"I don't have a bug and I surely don't have a temper."

"Surely," Audrey chuckled.

"But—I suspect if she was planning a party for your boyfriend due to mere obligation, she would have given you a little more notice, don't you think? God forbid, even include you in the preparations?"

"Include me? Ha! She is waiting on the sidelines for me to disappear so she can move in. But I don't care, I'm not worried about her. Besides, I wouldn't have time to do anything anyway. I have too much work to do." Seven out of the twelve pieces she'd created sold and the show had another five weeks left. Ben urged her to print replacements along with a few new images.

"Then, my friend, more power to you."

*

Traffic in L.A is a cancer, Audrey thought, surprisingly irritated at the prospect of not getting at the party before Jennifer had spread her tentacles all over John. She thought about what he'd said: everything they did lately kept them apart. He was right, of course. She tried so hard to not be labeled as a groupie so she didn't make an effort to stick to her job at Atlantis.

Her eyes swept the area when she exited the elevator at the top floor of the hotel. The rooftop was divided in two sections with the bar in the center. John, Tyler, Matt, Kevin, Jennifer and Bill were at one corner talking around a high top table with a bottle of champagne inside a frosted ice bucket. Audrey saw Tyler elbowing John and pointing in her direction. John detached himself from the group, leaving Jennifer with her mouth open mid-sentence. She held his gaze as he approached, giving her a subtle nod of his head and a gleeful smile.

"Happy Birthday, baby." She wrapped her arms around his neck, stood on her tiptoes and kissed him.

"You look amazing," he said, arms around her waist.

Audrey had worn the same outfit she did on their first date, down to the smoky eyes and black jewelry.

"Thanks. I don't believe you told me that the first time around."

"I couldn't speak then, I was too scared."

"Hmm. And you're not anymore?"

"Just a little."

"Scared of what?"

He whispered in her ear, "Of you not wanting to be my wife."

Her heart skipped a beat. "You don't have to fear that, I've already said yes." She kissed him. Then, he hugged her tighter and lifted off her feet. "Yes, yes."

"Yes, yes," Kevin said with mockery, peering at their faces as he moved toward them. "What's going on?" he asked.

John put Audrey down and turned to Kevin. "We're"—he looked at Audrey who nodded—"getting married."

"Oh yes, yes! That's awesome." Kevin ushered John and Audrey back to the table. "Let's have a toast."

Before they reached the table, Kevin shouted, "They're engaged!"

Matt and Tyler let out grunts of excitement, Bill grunted as well and, although Audrey couldn't read lips, she was certain it was "fuck" he muttered under his breath. Jennifer knocked back her flute of champagne and parted her lips in a muted smile.

At the table, Matt, Tyler, and even Jennifer hugged and congratulated them. Bill refrained from physical contact with Audrey but tapped John on the back and went to the bar to order another bottle of Dom Pérignon.

"Ahhh." When Megan arrived, she screamed so loud even blabbermouth Kevin looked abashed. "It's okay, I'm okay." She told the people staring. "My friend is getting married."

"Let me see the ring." Megan reached for Audrey's hand.

"I don't need a ring," Audrey said.

"Good for you." Tyler said. "If—and if is a big word here—I ask a girl to marry me, there will be no ring. I hate when the woman needs to look at the damn thing before she says yes or no."

"There is a ring. It's just not here," John said.

"Um, last minute decision. How romantic," Jennifer said.

"It wasn't last minute. I wanted this since the first time I laid my eyes on Audrey." John said with no hint of irony, his face stiff as a piece of oak.

Jennifer gave the slightest shrug and smiled sheepishly.

*

Sometime later, the other executives and producers from Atlantis had arrived and the party moved to a semi-private area near the pool. Orange cushioned seating spread the length of two walls that converged at the corner of the room. Jennifer arranged a birthday cake from a fancy Beverly Hills bakery famous for their rich chocolate flour-less cakes. A waitress with a big smile on her face brought it to the table, flickering candles on top. Later, the waitress asked the band to autograph a napkin while she cleared the glasses and beer bottles from the acrylic white tables in front of them.

On the dance floor, Megan and Matt moved to the never-ending stream of music the DJ put out. Kevin and Tyler talked to a group of girls who sat inside a red Hershey's kiss shaped pod. John was engaged in a discussion with Glenn and Bill about the lack of acoustic guitars in contemporary music.

"Where's Matt?" Audrey asked Megan when, minutes later, she sat on the orange couch beside Audrey.

"He went to get us drinks."

"So?" Audrey said conspiratorially. "Is he a contender for the body fluids exchange?" Audrey slid closer to Megan who snorted with her gaze averted. If Audrey didn't know better she would think Megan was embarrassed.

"Actually, he is pretty sweet," she said.

Jennifer must have eavesdropped on their conversation, because as soon as Megan closed her mouth she walked away from her group to intercept Matt who was coming from the bar with two glasses in his hands. Audrey and Megan watched as Jennifer smiled, tossed her hair to the side, and touched his forearm—apparently, her favorite moves.

"What's with that girl?" Megan repositioned herself on couch, clearly ticked off.

"I don't know." Audrey hoped Matt would know better than to fall for Jennifer's feigned interest. When Matt pointed his drinks in their direction and stepped away, Audrey let out a breath of relief and asked him, "What was that about?"

"Something about another party and if I wanted to go with her." Matt handed Megan her drink and took a sip of his. "I'm not going anywhere."

Later when the party dispersed, Audrey and John leaned against the white metal rail which circled the perimeter of the roof. For once, L.A. seemed peaceful. Angelical. She glanced at John surveying the immensity of the city. Not long ago, she was small and lonely, now she felt important because he'd chosen to share his life with her.

"When I got in that bus seven months ago, I could never have imagined I would be here tonight—with you." She turned to face him. "I've never believed things happened because they were meant to . . . I was so scared to make the wrong choices and end up living a life I've never signed up for. But since that night in Augusta, when you brought me a Snickers bar and smiled." Her voice stumbled around the word smiled. "I knew all the decisions I would make from then on would be because of you."

John gently kissed her lips and said, "A Snicker's bar, huh?" He moved an unruly strand of hair off her face. "I have to remember that."

*

Light seeped through the windows of their bedroom when John drew open the curtains the next day.

"You already up?" She stretched her arms. "What time is it?"

"About ten." He sat on the bed and kissed her. "I want to give you something." Between his fingers a delicate engagement ring with a split-pea sized diamond guarded by two soft pink stones set in polished white gold. "It arrived a few days ago. I asked my father to send it to me."

"Wow." Audrey whispered, propping herself on her elbows.

"I wanted to plan something romantic—"

"Like, maybe, writing a song?"

"Maybe." He chuckled. "But I couldn't help myself yesterday."

"It's beautiful."

"It was my mother's. She gave it to me before she died."

"Oh, John."

"I didn't wanted it . . . I told her no one in the world could deserve it. She told me I would find someone." His voice dropped to a murmur. "And when I did, I should let her in. Not be so serious. So stubborn." He stared at the ring in his hand.

"She must've loved you very much." She sat up and caressed his face.

He held her gaze and said, "I didn't believe her—until now." He scooted closer and took her hand. "Audrey . . . love of my life. You make me so happy."—He slid the ring on her finger—"You're the one for me. The woman I've never believed existed."—He tenderly kissed her hand—"Will you marry me?"

Chapter 26

The courtyard of the small restaurant off Sunset Boulevard was cobbled. The feel of the smooth bumps beneath the soles of Audrey's shoes reminded her of the farm in Brazil. Her grandfather and uncles had hauled hundreds of cobble stones in a wheelbarrow to create a trail connecting the main house to the outside kitchen. Audrey thought it was odd to have a kitchen outside the house, but she learned it was not uncommon in the rural areas of Brazil. It was actually very logical. Her mother had explained they cooked mainly with a wood stove and the smoke would impregnate everything inside the house.

"And your grandpa would bring mud into the house every time he came in to have a drink of his Jurubeba." Audrey's grandmother had told her in Portuguese.

Audrey's grandfather was lean and tanned from walking the land, doing task after task until the sun went down. During the day, he would make several stops in the kitchen to pour himself a dose of the dark liquid into a tin cup that remained always on top of the bottle. Once he let Audrey taste it, laughing while she twisted her face and stuck her tongue out.

"It's medicine." He had told her.

"*Não é não.*" It's not. She'd told him with no hint of accent. For her, medicine was pink and tasted like bubble gum.

Bitter and spicy, the liquid was an herbal concoction made with cloves, cinnamon, wine and the extract from the jurubeba plant. Supposedly, it strengthened the weak stomach and cured inflammations of the liver and spleen. It also had a seventeen percent volume of alcohol, which was the medicinal benefit her grandfather seemed to prize most.

"Audrey." Megan waved her hand from a corner table.

"Hi, I'm sorry. Have you been waiting long?" She sat across from Megan and threw her purse on an empty chair.

"No. Ten minutes tops."

"I lost track of time in the darkroom."

"How is it going?"

"I've finished the reprints, now I'm working on the new ones."

The waitress brought water, took their order, and hurriedly walked away, as if the restaurant was packed, when in fact, there were only other two tables occupied.

"That's cool. Then you'll be able to go to London."

"I don't think so. They leave in two days, and I won't be able to finish it by then."

"Are you serious? It's their first concert abroad, it's a big deal." Megan said.

"I know exactly how important this is." She took a sip from the glass of water in front of her.

"You finished the show replacements, right?"

"Right."

"Then?"

Audrey remained quiet.

"You've fulfilled your commitment," Megan said.

"Well—" Audrey waited for the waitress to place their salad plates on the table. "I did, but I still have to print the new images he's asked for."

Megan shook her head and ferried a forkful of lettuce to her mouth.

"Besides, my passport is at my parents," Audrey said.

"Big deal. Have you heard of FEDEX?"

"I don't know. I just. . . ." Her voice trailed off.

"Listen, I understand you didn't want to be the center of attention when 'North Star' came out. And you didn't want people to think you're sponging off and sleeping with the whole band."

Audrey creased her eyebrows.

"But you're going to marry the guy now. Who cares what people think anymore?"

"It's not about what people think."

"What is it then, Audrey?" Megan put her fork down. "Because I'd love to know why you're going to put an ocean between you and John, so the Edwards and Jennifers of the world can come between the two of you?"

Audrey slumped in her chair. "John is a wonderful musician. I know he'll do well. I just want to do the same." She sighed. "It took me a long time to find something I could see myself doing for the rest of my life. I don't want to give it up."

"Sweetie." Megan touched Audrey's hand. "You don't have to give it up. You're an artist; it's within you. You don't need a gallery in North Hollywood to make art." Megan snorted. "You certainly don't need Ben. Can you believe he called me a sweet bun at the show opening?"

"Absolutely," Audrey smiled.

"You know . . . Matt asked me to go with them." Megan gave her a witty grin.

"Really? Are you guys . . . why didn't you tell me?"

Megan shrugged.

"How? When? It was at John's party, wasn't it?"

"We didn't sleep together that night, so you know," Megan said.

Audrey giggled at Megan's newfound self-righteousness.

"We just talked and danced. He is so funny." Megan's eyes sparkled. "He asked if I wanted to go to the movies the next day. I said yes. We made out in his car when he dropped me off."

"Oh, how sweet."

"It really was." Megan mused. "It had been a while since I had a proper date. Usually, you sleep with a guy and, if you like him, hope he'll call the next day. If you don't, just try to forget it ever happened."

"You said a mouthful there, sister." The waitress, bringing the dessert menu, winked at Megan.

Audrey and Megan laughed and ordered crème brûlée to split, and two espressos. When the waitress left, Audrey turned to Megan with an inquisitive gaze.

"So, on our second date," Megan said. "Third, really, if you count the party. We went back to the hotel and got a room—our places are so crowded."

"I am happy for both of you."

"Thanks. And guess what?" Megan beamed in a smile. "He called the next day."

"Of course he did." Audrey was the one now who lightly touched Megan's hand. "Matt is a smart man."

The waitress arrived with their dessert and coffee.

"Are you going, then?" Audrey asked.

"I can't. It's the middle of the semester. I can't miss classes."

"Oh."

"But you can go, Audrey. Please! Please!" Megan said, with her mouth full of crème brûlée. "Go stay with your"—she singsonged—"fiancé. And remember: it also took you a long time to find someone you wanted to do for the rest of your life." Megan winked.

*

Audrey loved the day after a gig, when John could stay home. Even he, a morning person almost to the point of annoyance, would succumb to her pleas and stay in bed for as long as she wanted. At two in the afternoon, they decided to have pancakes for lunch. Golden, fluffy discs sat piled up on a plate while John placed juice, fruit, and syrup on the table. He fixed their coffee, cream and sugar for him, and black for her. Then he ambled up behind Audrey and placed her cup on the counter beside the stove, his free hand circling her waist.

"Thank you." She tipped her head back against his chest.

"You're welcome." He pulled her hair to the side and gently kissed her ear and her neck.

"This way I'm going to burn our breakfast."

"I think we have enough anyway." John glanced at the tall stack on the plate.

"You think so?"

"Unless the rest of the band is coming over."

She turned off the stove, tilted the pan and dropped the last pancake on top of the stack. John sat at the table and she followed, bringing the plate and her coffee mug.

"I wanted to wait for you last night because I've been meaning to tell you something." Audrey had tried to stay awake, but her feet and back ached from the long hours standing in the darkroom.

"Uh?" John forked a pancake and dropped it into his plate.

"I'd like to go with you to London, if you'd still take me."

"Are you serious?"

"Uh-huh." She gulped her coffee.

"Hell, yeah. That's great."

"Do you think I can still get into the same flight?"

"I think so. I'll call Atlantis right away." He stood up.

"No, John. It can wait. Have breakfast with me." Audrey placed her hand on top of his.

A few minutes later, John's cell rang from the bedroom.

"I should get it." He said sheepishly.

"Okay, I'm finished anyway. Can't eat anymore." She pushed her cleaned plate away.

"It's Tyler." He shouted from the bedroom.

Audrey stood and topped her coffee. She met John in the living room, his face suddenly pale.

"We'll be right there." John hung up the phone. "Something is wrong with Kevin."

Chapter 27

When they arrived at the apartment complex, an ambulance, a fire truck, and two police cars were on the street. John didn't bother parking the car properly and they ran to the apartment. The door was wide open. Matt and Tyler stood in the living room. Matt's eyes were puffed and red and he had his arms crossed in front of him, and Tyler was pressing with his fingers on the bridge of his nose. Two police officers stood in front of them, one with a hand on Tyler's shoulder.

For an instant, Audrey heard a deafening buzz in her ears and everything seemed to be in slow motion. John froze in front of her, staring at Matt and Tyler. Her steps sounded heavy on the carpet, running to the bedroom. When she reached the door, she saw Kevin lying on the bed. Someone grabbed her and blocked her from coming in.

"Get off me, he's my friend." She shouted at the police officer and with the strength she didn't know she had, jerked herself out of his grasp and ran to the bed.

She touched Kevin's face; his skin was cool and sticky. His blond hair spilled on the bed like a puddle of golden blood. His T-shirt was cut open, his still chest marked by the defibrillator the paramedic on the other side of the bed was stowing into a case

"Kevin? Kevin, wake up!" She shook his shoulder.

Audrey glanced up at the paramedic, but the woman looked down, avoiding her gaze.

"No." She touched her face to his and sobbed.

Hands were pulling her again, but this time she recognized them. John helped her up and they hugged and cried for a long time.

*

There was a bite of cold in the air on the Thursday morning of Kevin's funeral. He would've liked the scenery, she thought. Surrounded by fall's golden trees, the cemetery had a bleak film noir feeling worthy of Hitchcock. For an instant, Kevin's image flashed through her mind; him smoking a cigar, drinking whiskey, and watching The Twilight Zone in a cheap hotel room. The memory was as vivid as it had just happened yesterday, but their life had changed so much, it could have been another lifetime.

The tears rolled down thick on his mother's face. She let out a deep sob every few minutes, gasping for air as if someone had covered her head with a plastic bag and tied it firmly around her neck. She had auburn hair and her skin was so pale, it seemed to have been bleached by sorrow. Kevin had taken after his father, who was lean and tall, but he had his mother's eyes—piercing green with swatches of yellow, like orbs of jade.

Kevin had a big family; two married older sisters with five children between them and a younger brother. Many uncles, aunts, and cousins forming a thick wall of tears and grief stood behind his parents. Even the younger children seemed to sit uncharacteristically still, listening to the minister's words.

John looked glum, shoulders curled toward his chest. He didn't talk much, especially about Kevin. He was the one who made the call to Kevin's parents, and now it was as if he had used up all the words.

"There has been an accident," John had told Kevin's father.

After what Audrey assumed was Kevin's father asking if his son was okay, John said "He has passed...I'm so sorry." John cupped his mouth and held the tears as he explained to Mr. Everhart what the police had told them earlier. "We found him in his bedroom, he wasn't breathing. The police found lots of prescription medicine in his room. They think he accidentally overdosed." He was crying when he continued telling Mr. Everhart that no one in the band suspected he was taking any medicine or even had seen him going to a doctor. He'd told him Kevin drank, but he didn't say anything about his cocaine use or the incident in Ryan Correll's house.

No matter what John said, the truth was that he felt responsible for Kevin's death, the same way he felt responsible for everyone's well-being. The nights before Audrey and John flew to the funeral in Illinois, she'd found him on the backyard's bench smoking in the dark. She didn't know how to comfort him, because she also felt as if she'd failed Kevin. So, they sat on the dark, close but not quite touching.

Bill and Jennifer released statements on the behalf of the band and Atlantis, respectively. Once again, gossip magazines and paparazzi had taken interest, and they wrote wildly about Kevin's short Hollywood life. The models he dated, the parties he attended, even mentioned a falling-out with his famous friend Ryan Correll because of a mystery girl. The press alluded to suicide and drug abuse. Not long before Kevin's death, two actors, a man and a woman about the same age as Kevin, had also died suddenly due to their exploitations with prescribed medication and, allegedly, illicit drugs. A national morning show brought in a psychiatrist to talk about the wave of young celebrities who perish under the pressures of their famous lives.

After the funeral, the family gathered in Kevin's parents' house. Audrey sat on the stairwell to the second floor, playing Uno with some of the children. She looked over the living room and John, Tyler and Matt were talking with Kevin's father. Mrs. Everhart had gone upstairs to lay down, ushered by her daughters. John hung his head low, hands on the pockets of his suit pants. Mr. Everhart lifted his hand and placed on John's shoulders, then embraced him.

The scene was like a movie, the prodigal son had returned home. Except John was repentant, but not his son. Mr. Everhart's boy would never come back. Audrey's eyes welled up, and the two little girls of distinct blond curls that were strangely familiar to her stared and waited for her to place a card on the pile. A wild card.

Chapter 28

When the airplane touched the tarmac at LAX, Audrey let out a long breath. Nauseated and hot, she squeezed her thighs with her sweaty hands and prayed to heavens reaching the terminal wouldn't take long. From the next seat, John reached for her hand and tightly braided his fingers on hers. They looked at each other, and he managed to give her a faint smile that brought solace with it. He looked vulnerable, his sunken eyes stunned by the rupture created by Kevin's death. For her, that simple touch was a sign of a coma patient regaining consciousness.

They drove home in silence, Matt and Tyler followed in their car. Since the accident they hadn't returned to their apartment. Jennifer had hired movers to take their stuff to the bungalow. Luckily, Matt and Tyler had rented their furniture, so the bungalow's spare bedroom and garage had more than enough space for their personal belongings. Kevin's clothes were donated to charity and everything else was sent to his parents. For once, Audrey felt thankful for Atlantis—and Jennifer—for taking care of all of it.

Bill had flown into town the same day to hold meetings with Atlantis's executives about the band's future. For the past months, they had been promoting their first album and performing. Unsure of their profitability, Atlantis hadn't renewed their contract yet. John had told Audrey he hoped Atlantis would agree on renewing their contract with Kevin as their lead singer, since he hadn't caused any more trouble. The concerts in London, which were supposed to determine their fate, had been canceled.

At home, Audrey sipped tea and the boys drank coffee. She still felt queasy from the trip and coffee was more than what her stomach could handle at that moment. A few hours later, Megan arrived, tender and respectfully quiet. Matt and Megan held each other for long minutes, and they looked sweet together. Underneath the foul mouth and the apparent detachment, Megan was a romantic who was swept away by Matt's chivalry and kindness.

"May I come in?" Megan gently knocked on the door of Audrey's bedroom.

"Of course. I'm only unpacking."

"How are you?"

"I'm okay, I guess. It's weird being back without Kevin."

"I can imagine."

"Where's Matt?"

"He went for cigarettes with John and Tyler."

"Um." Audrey nodded absently while folding one of John's T-shirts.

"So, what's going to happen next?" Megan sat on the bed.

"I don't know."

"Do you think they'll go on?"

"Atlantis demanded to have Kevin off the band for the second album."

"Really?"

"Yeah. I assume at one point they must have—at least—considered the possibility."

"Matt won't say it, but I feel he'll do whatever John decides."

"I have no idea what John will do. Music is his life, but he is shaken."

The doorbell rang.

"John must've forgotten his key." Audrey threw a pair of jeans on the bed and went to open the door.

"Oh, Bill," Audrey said with a miffed air and walked to the kitchen where Megan was getting a bottle of water from the fridge.

"Hello Audrey." Bill stepped in. "Are the boys home?"

"No."

"Where are they?"

"Not sure." She said without looking at him.

"Okay, I'll wait." Bill opened a button of his suit and plopped himself on the couch.

"Who is he?" Megan mouthed to Audrey when she walked into the kitchen.

Audrey whispered, "their manager." Filling the coffee pot with water, she asked Megan, "Do you want some coffee?"

"I'd love some, thanks." Bill hollered from his seat.

"I wasn't talking to you," Audrey said.

Only then, Bill seemed to realize someone else was there. He turned his neck and saw Megan leaning against the counter while Audrey gathered the ingredients.

"Oh, hi there," he said.

"Hi." Megan waved faintly.

"I'm Bill . . . but I'm sure Audrey must have told you all about me."

"Don't flatter yourself," Audrey said.

"I want you to know I've never had anything against you—personally." He got up and stopped on the threshold between living room and kitchen.

"Oh, how kind." Against her facial muscles, Audrey curled up the corner of her lips.

"It's not good business to split your energy between starting a new relationship and a new career." He spoke matter-of-factly.

"And what makes you the expert—your stellar career or your sterling marriage?" Audrey regarded Bill with profound disdain. He closed his eyes and massaged the bridge of his nose.

Turning from the coffee maker to face him, she said, "You were just terrified to lose your control over John to me, but what you didn't understand was that no one controls him. You'd know it if your head wasn't stuck so far up your ass." She slammed the coffee cups on the counter. Megan, looking like she was enjoying the show, sat at the table.

"I guess this isn't a good time to make amends." Bill wound his way back to the living room. As he slouched into the futon, the door opened and John, Matt, and Tyler walked in.

"Hey, guys." Bill got to his feet.

"Hi, Bill," Matt said. John and Tyler nodded.

"We need to talk." Bill clasped his hands together.

John and Matt emptied grocery bags on the kitchen counter. Tyler had sat on the chair across from Bill and jammed his hands in his armpits.

"Is that fresh coffee?" Matt rubbed Megan's shoulder.

"Yes, sir." Audrey propped her elbows at the table and clasped her mug with her hands. John leaned over and kissed her, his lips lingering over hers for a long moment.

"I'd love some," Bill said tentatively from the living room.

Audrey and Megan exchanged glances.

"I'll fix you a cup," Matt volunteered.

"Is everything okay?" John asked Audrey, still leaning over her. "Splendid."

Audrey turned to Megan. "Do you want to go for a walk?"

"Please don't leave," John said.

Audrey got up and took her cup to the sink. "I don't think it's our place—"

"It's fine. This won't take long." He gave her hand a light squeeze and walked to the living room.

"What's up, Bill?" John said.

Matt handed Bill a cup of coffee.

"We've been through a terrible tragedy." Bill glanced around the room. "Kevin will be deeply missed, but I'm sure he'd like us to continue—"

"We're done, Bill," John said.

"What?" Bill's eyes widened.

"That's it. No more band." Tyler spoke without lifting his gaze.

Bill turned to Matt who nodded in agreement.

"This is ridiculous. I just had news from Atlantis, you don't need Kevin . . . I mean, John can sing." He placed his mug on the coffee table and wiped his forehead with his hand. "It will be poetic."

John shook his head. "You have no idea what you're talking about."

"What the hell." Bill paced in front of the couch. "Matt, Tyler what are you going to do? Are you going to let him destroy your careers?"

"Hey, we only play the instruments. A lot of people can do that," Matt said.

"John, I know you're upset right now, but this is a mistake." Bill's voice was pleading. "You're engaged. How are you going to support your family?"

"I don't believe that's any of your concern."

"What's going on here? Are you going solo? That's it, isn't it?" Bill turned around and rubbed his chin. "I'm sorry pal, but you can't do that. You have a contract."

"We're aware of our contract, Bill. I suspect Atlantis won't go through the trouble of finding a lead singer for a band that has only a few months left."

"I see."

"There's one more thing." John took a step closer to Bill. "Your services are no longer needed."

Audrey's mouth fell open, and so did Bill's.

"You're fired," John said.

"Huh?" Bill snorted. "You can't fire me."

"I just did."

Audrey covered her mouth, struggling to not burst out laughing. Megan squeezed her hand and shushed her. Bill looked at Matt and Tyler who stared back at him silently.

"After all we've been through?"

"After all we've been through?" John intoned. "Tell me Bill, what is it you've done that accomplished any of this?"

"I arranged the tour."

"Merely half of it. The other gigs John booked himself," Tyler said.

"You've met her because of the tour." Bill waved his hand toward the kitchen.

John chuckled and looked at Audrey, then turned back to Bill. "Oh, yeah. Sorry, I forgot you were responsible for fate."

*

Later that night, the house was quiet. After Bill stormed out swearing it wasn't the last time they would hear from him, Matt and Megan went to the movies and Tyler left to meet some of the people he befriended at Atlantis. Audrey walked in the bedroom and found John sitting on the bed, stroking softly his acoustic guitar.

"Are you okay?" She asked, sitting across from him at the edge of the bed.

"I'm fine." He gave her a thin smile.

"John." She sighed and said, "Are you sure this is what you want? You've worked so hard—"

"I'm sure."

"It just seemed so sudden."

"It isn't, really. It's, uh, cumulative." He propped his guitar against the night stand. "I was young and all I've wanted was to play. After my mother died, it was all I had. I got older and I still just wanted to play; but then, everything got complicated, you have to make a living, and there's all this expectation."

"Climbing on the bandwagon," she said, half to herself.

She knew exactly what he meant, she'd felt carried by the current of living as a responsible adult before: setting goals, making money, having a career which were all great if she'd known what she wanted to do with her life all along. Her art history degree had only set her on the right trail.

"This life is not what I wanted, you know?"

"Of course. I just don't want you to have any regrets."

"I won't." He extended his hand to her, then pulled her close. "I have you."

She sat sideways between his legs and rested her head on his chest, and said, "What will you do?"

"I'll do whatever as long as we're together."

"How about music?"

"I'm not going to stop making music, but I refuse to sell out so Atlantis can make more profit." He tightened his arms around her. "I've been thinking of what you've said. About school?"

Sometime after Audrey discovered she wanted to pursue art as a career, she started to think she finally might go back to school to get a MFA.

"And?"

"I think I'd also like to give graduate school a try, uh…" His voice dropped to a murmur. "Back in Illinois."

Audrey stared deeply into his amber eyes, and said, "Sounds perfect."

Epilogue

Pumpkin spice scent filled Audrey's parents' house on the day of her wedding. Due to Isabel's insistence, Audrey agreed to have an intimate ceremony at her parents' house. It was only appropriate, it hadn't been two months since Kevin's death. Audrey suggested they waited a bit longer, but John wanted to get married as soon as possible.

"Did I knock you up? What's the hurry?" Audrey had asked him one night when, while spooning in bed, he suggested eloping to Las Vegas.

"I want to start new, with you as my wife."

She'd melt every time he said "my wife," but she never cared for the fluffy-white-gown and bridesmaids-by-the-dozen shenanigans. City Hall would have been fine, but her mother insisted on doing something—anything. She agreed, as long as her parents promised to respect her guest list and the ceremony could be performed by a non-denominational minister.

The party planning company her parents hired attached poles to the ground, then loosely draped pearlescent gossamer panels around, creating a sheer tent. Its back wall was a fall-inspired wedding arch, with sunflowers, seeded eucalyptus, curly willow, and large burgundy roses.

Before leaving L.A., Megan had helped her pick out the dress, an ivory empire waist strapless with a thin taupe ribbon.

"But it's a bridesmaid's dress." Marjorie, the wedding-gown specialist at the store, had protested when Audrey pulled the dress from a 50 percent discount rack.

Megan giggled and sipped the complimentary champagne Marjorie had served them after Audrey told her she was looking for a wedding gown. Audrey handed Marjorie the bridesmaid dress to place in the fitting room. Marjorie gave Megan an insufferable look as if that dress didn't even pay for the champagne she wasted on them.

"This will do." Audrey twirled in front of the mirror checking her reflection with the same enthusiasm of someone trying on scrubs.

"Oh, you're such a romantic. It touches me," Megan said.

"You know I would wear jeans and boots if I could. I'm doing this for my mom." Audrey pulled the already half-open zipper down.

"You should be doing this for your daughter." Megan had tilted her glass up, sucking the last drop of champagne, for Marjorie was unlikely to relinquish any more.

"What?" Audrey turned to Megan.

"Imagine you'll have a daughter someday and she'll want to see her mommy's wedding pictures. You'll be happy you didn't wear jeans and boots," she sighed, "or a tankini."

"Ha. Was that what your mother wore?"

Nodding sheepishly, Megan said, "She got married in Key West."

"Aw, that is romantic."

Megan had come to Illinois to spend Thanksgiving with Matt. They had been dating exclusively and seemed to be walking steadily toward living together. Matt and Tyler had decided to remain in L.A. and take over the bungalow. Tyler was hired as an in-house musician at Atlantis, a position Audrey didn't know existed. Matt did the same, substituting for other musicians as needed, but on a freelance basis because of his new job as a software developer at Apple.

Audrey and John were renting a house in Illinois, which made Isabel very happy. L.A. would still be a part of their life, since Glenn was interested in several of John's songs which John had decided he didn't want to record for himself. Glenn insisted John would come to L.A. when necessary to produce the songs with him. Audrey would accompany him whenever she needed to see Ben, who had booked her a solo show in the Spring.

Isabel steamed the dress while Audrey watched the tent being set up from her window. John had taken his suit and toiletry bag to the spare bedroom to get ready. He'd been a little embarrassed when Isabel had shown them to Audrey's room the night before.

"Are we in the same room?" He'd muttered when Isabel left.

"Does it offend your maidenhood?"

"Your parents are right down the hall."

"We were in the same room at your dad's."

"It's just . . . I don't know."

"Don't worry, Dad knows you're marrying me tomorrow."

At night, Audrey had tickled him under the covers while he shushed her nervously and pleaded for silence.

"How about a last lay as a single guy?" She'd slid her hands under his undershirt. "You can pretend it's your bachelor party and I can give you a lap dance." But John refused to make love to her with her parents sleeping down the hall. At least, not before they were married. She'd called him square, but truthfully, she thought it was endearing. She'd lain on her side and John curled around her facing her back.

"Good night, sweet almost-wife o' mine," he'd said into her neck.

A soft knock on the door brought Audrey back to reality and she turned from the window.

"Come in."

"Hello there." Megan pushed the door.

"Megan." Audrey stepped closer and gave her a hug. "Did you just arrive?"

"Yes. Matt is downstairs talking to John."

"John is down there already?"

"Uh-huh. Looking pretty sharp in a brown suit."

"Dressed?"

"Something about getting claustrophobic alone in the bedroom." Megan turned to Isabel. "Hi, Mrs. Whitman."

"Hi darling." Isabel hung Audrey's dress on a hook in the closet and gave Megan a hug.

"You should be getting ready. The minister is here," Megan said.

"Oh, I should go talk to him. Megan can help you get ready." Isabel nodded at Megan.

"Yes, of course." Megan nodded back.

Isabel returned to the room with a hat box, from which she pulled a bouquet that matched the wedding arch, with deep red roses, delicate freesias, and other gold and orange colored flowers tightly tied together by a burgundy ribbon.

"Mom, it's beautiful." Audrey hugged and kissed her mom. "Thank you so much—for everything." Her eyes welled up.

"Oh, my girl." Isabel cupped Audrey's face in her hands. "You deserve everything. I know you'll be so happy."

They held each other tight until Isabel loosened the embrace and said, "You look beautiful. Now what to do with the hair?"

"I don't know. Maybe I'll just have it down." Audrey looked at Isabel and Megan and they shook their heads.

Megan pulled out a small paper bag from her purse and handed to Audrey. "I saw these the other day and thought of you." It was a package of filigree hair pins in a lotus design with tiny rhinestones at the tip of each petal.

"These are great. Thank you." Audrey handed the package to her mom.

"Come sweetie, sit down." Isabel told Audrey. "How about if we pull this much up..." She propped some of Audrey's hair up on the crown of her head. "And leave the rest down, cascading on one shoulder?"

"Perfect," Audrey said.

"I'll get the curling iron." Megan vanished into the bathroom.

When they opened the door of the bedroom thirty minutes later, Audrey's father was waiting at the top of the stairs.

"Oh, angel. You look beautiful." George stepped up and gave Audrey a kiss on the cheeks.

"Thanks, Daddy."

"See you out there." Megan squeezed by Audrey and her parents and headed down the stairs.

"I'll let them know you're ready." Isabel followed Megan.

George squeezed Audrey's hand and ushered her downstairs. From the French doors that led to the backyard, she could see the guests through the sheer fabric: Steve and—finally—a date his own age, Tyler, Charlie, John's father and brothers, and her parents. The four blurred shapes standing in front of the rows of chairs were Matt and Megan as the best man and maid-of-honor, the minister, and John. Audrey held John's gaze as she crossed the yard holding her father's arm.

A familiar sound came from the small speakers tied inconspicuously to the ginkgo tree: an instrumental version of "North Star." Audrey, still staring at John, smiled. Looking surprised, he turned to Matt, who shrugged and tilted his head toward Tyler, who was grinning triumphantly. For a moment, Audrey saw Kevin sitting on one of the white chairs. Cheery and beautiful, with his wide smile narrowing his eyes so the only thing you could see was a hint of acid green melting gloominess away. Then the moment was gone. She looked back at John and took another step toward the future.

*

After one week of romantic dinners, sightseeing, and sunbathing lazily on the beaches of Rio de Janeiro, Audrey and John took the short flight to Goiânia.

"It seems my entire family is here," Audrey said looking past the exit doors.

"Wow." He looked at the multitude of people closing in on them when they'd exited the baggage claim area.

Hugs and kisses, handshakes and taps on the shoulders went around punctuated by Portuguese and broken English. She looked at John and laughed, as his widened eyes gave away his first cultural shock. She was sure he'd never been so warmly greeted, not even when the band was at the peak of their popularity.

Five cars made the procession to the farm. Audrey's aunt, Janny, drove them. Audrey enunciated her name, "zh ⊠ nē," so John could learn the pronunciation.

"You can call me Jane. I always thought it sounded cool." She smiled at John from the rearview mirror.

Her little boy sat beside John on the backseat and proudly counted to ten in English to show him how smart he was. John taught him to count to twenty, and Lucas counted over and over until he fell asleep a few minutes into the ride.

After driving for forty minutes, they turned on a dirt road and spiraled down for three miles. Audrey felt the temperature dropping as they got close to the river that cut through her family's land. Her cousin jumped out of the car in front of them and opened the heavy wooden gate. They bounced as the car passed through a cattle-guard.

The house of her mother's childhood sat on top of a slight hill, stained and tattered by time, yet warm and cozy with memories. The cars parked in a crooked line near the chicken wire fence surrounding the house and yard, and she could see flames twinkling in the wood stove in the outdoors kitchen.

She was surprised by the overwhelming feeling of peace expanding in her chest. For over a decade, she'd ignored Isabel's pleas to come to Brazil. She had even resented the love her mother had for the farm. Audrey had never seen her displaying so much happiness in the U.S. as she did here. Secretly, she feared her mother would leave to go to Brazil and never come back, but when John squeezed her hand, she understood why Isabel had never left them. As she stood in front of the house, surrounded by mango trees, she felt a deep tenderness for her mother. I've never gotten it, Mom. She looked at John and smiled. But now I do.

"Let's get some mangos." She pulled him toward a giant mango tree near the side of the house and behind the ruins of a cement shed.

"I've never seen a mango tree before. It's huge."

"Cool, uh?"

Under the tree, Audrey pointed at a mango and jumped to grab it, but it was beyond her reach. John plucked it out with one jump and gave it to her. The branches bounced like a ripple in a lake. Then, he grabbed one for himself.

"What now?" He looked at Audrey, then at the fruit in his hand.

"You bite." Audrey carved her teeth into the mango and pulled out a piece of skin in one motion. She spit out the skin and bit the fleshy yellow meat, the sweet taste of her past blending with the hopes for her future filled her mouth. She closed her eyes and inhaled the sweet smell around her, wanting to engrave this feeling of peace and contentment into her heart forever. Then, she looked at John, who was staring at her with a mystified smile, and raised her eyebrows. He understood and dug in.

www.ingramcontent.com/pod-product-compliance
Lightning Source LLC
Chambersburg PA
CBHW010637100726
47900CB00011B/2869